THE MAN IN
THE MIDDLE

THE MAN IN THE MIDDLE

DAVID WAGONER

ISBN: 978-1-954841-82-6

Published by
Brash Books
PO Box 8212
Calabasas, CA 91372
www.brash-books.com

This book is dedicated to E. N., P. T., M. C. and September 25th

This minute I was well, and am ill, this minute. I am surpriz'd with a sodaine change, and alteration to worse, and can impute it to no cause, nor call it by any name.

—John Donne

CHAPTER ONE

Charlie Bell, the crossing tender, found no fault with the evening. The sun had reddened and gone behind the grain elevators and steel mills of South Chicago as usual, and the wind from the lake blew no sand across the dozen sets of tracks, to get into his eyes, to choke him. No cars had jounced over the tracks to the weedy park and beach for the last fifteen minutes, and only one more fast train would come through. After that, he could quit for the day and go home.

But he found fault with himself, sitting with his back against the watchman's shanty, looking at his spade-shaped warning sign propped in the cinders.

This was no kind of life. He hated the trains, hated the way they rumbled, shot steam, clanged. He stared beyond the ditches and the heaps of ties at the way the pale, reflected sunlight still creased the trees along the beach and lit the bricks of the filtration plant. He didn't want to watch the trains in the dark any more. Too much black, too much fire, now that he was no longer helping them run. They still had all the power and guts, but they had turned against him. He'd never felt so skinny before.

The red lights blinked on, and the bells on each side of the crossing started to ring. He got up, grabbed his sign, and stood in the middle of the road beside the first tracks. He watched the small diesel engine hum past, no cars behind it, and he waved half-heartedly at the switchman who sat on the scoop with a lantern. The bells stopped, and the lights went out. Both his legs started to ache at once, and he limped back to the shanty, trailing the sign behind him like a flattened-out hoe. He sat on the bench, his shins throbbing all the way down into his safety shoes.

Pulling out his gold watch, he saw that it was 7:33 Standard Time. Less than half an hour left. Maybe he could cut off a few minutes. His watch chain rustled against his vest, and he knew, if he tried, he could make it reach all the way around his ribs, like a tape measure. He waited for the wind to rise, as it always did, bringing the smell of fish, crude oil, and sewage. It was almost as punctual as a train or a sunset.

Without even knowing he was listening, he stood up in time to see the 7:36 for Chicago coming slowly down the blurred tracks where Gary burned red under its own reflection. He went out to the middle of the road. The train was coming too slowly, and when he looked back over his shoulder, he saw the high redboard telling it to wait. Must be some switching mix-up down the line.

The engine, chugging and snorting, pulled abreast of him, going no more than ten miles an hour, and the ground under him rocked with the hard surge of the pistons. The bell of the train and its steam, the crossing warning bells, and the clacketing of the wheels over the rail joints filled his ears and shook him. He turned aside and waited, not waving to anyone.

As the last car passed, Charlie, suddenly turning with it, saw that the upper half of the forward door was open, and while he watched, a woman, dressed in a gray suit, leaned out. She had a briefcase in one hand and was banging at the inside of the bottom door with the other. She turned, holding the briefcase outside the car, and he saw someone was hitting her in the face and grabbing at her arm. The end of the train moved down the track, forty feet, then fifty, sixty feet from him, and the woman was bent backward, hanging outside from the waist up.

He took a few steps along the tie-butts and started to run after the train, but his legs hurt and he remembered he wasn't supposed to run. He dropped his sign and kept walking.

The train still moved slowly, approaching the high line of red-eyes, and even in the dim light, Charlie could see the woman get hit in the face again, this time very hard. She did a raggedy backward somersault over the edge of the door and sprawled face down in the bank of cinders below, tossing the briefcase out to one side as she went. It flipped open in mid-air, and a flock of papers spilled out, caught in the puffs of wind from over the top of the train, and scattered between the rails, down to the roadbed, and into the clumps of weeds. The signal changed and, gathering speed, the train jerked ahead to pass a line of dead freight cars.

Charlie saw a man leaning out of the doorway with one leg over the ledge, looking straight at him, but the train was moving a little faster now and the boxcars were too close to let him jump.

The woman was on her hands and knees in the cinders, trying to get up. When Charlie put his hand under her arm to help her, she cried aloud and rolled away from him.

He said, "Just wait a second. Don't hurt yourself any more."

She was bleeding from the mouth, and when she pulled back her upper lip to cry, he saw that one of her teeth had been chipped off near the gum. The metal temples of her glasses were bent and caught in her hair. Her forehead, cheeks, and eyelids had been cut by the broken lenses.

She coughed and sobbed. "Who are you?"

"Crossing watchman. I saw you get drubbed out of the train." He helped her to her feet now, and she let him. Her clothes were smudged and torn by the sharp cinders, her stockings were shredded, and she held out her hands for both of them to see: they were scraped raw and embedded with slag. He took off her glasses and tossed them away.

She said, "The briefcase. Very important." She started to put her hands to her tangled hair, but then she didn't. She stood, swaying on the tilted embankment, and crossed her arms over her stomach.

Charlie said, "You never mind about that. I'll pick the stuff up." He steered her down to the level ground and aimed her toward the crossing. "You start walking along there."

She took a few unsteady steps, then turned half around, holding her hands limp across her breasts. "I can't see hardly at all. My glasses."

"Just walk a little bit. Slow." Charlie picked up the briefcase from where it had slid into a small puddle. It was still half full of papers. He picked up all he could see from around the rails, found a few more pigeonholed between the ends of the ties, then scouted the nearby weeds for the rest. Some of them were small and looked like pictures of checks, but he didn't try to read any. He was thinking about the man on the train. He tried to remember how long the string of freights was. He'd seen them go by earlier in the day and put into that siding. The man couldn't have jumped out till he got past them, not if he knew what was healthy. Charlie put it at about two hundred yards. He looked down the tracks and couldn't even see the tail sign of the train any more. And probably by that time, it would have been going fast enough to make jumping very unpleasant. You could never tell, though. At least, he couldn't spot anyone coming toward him from the direction of Chicago.

He picked up the last piece of paper he could see. It was getting dark rapidly, and the white oblongs didn't show very sharply. He walked around a bit longer, but when he turned toward his shanty and saw that the woman was sitting in the roadbed only a dozen yards away, he gave up and snapped the leather case shut.

Catching up with her, he supported her with one arm, and they limped together back to the crossing where the streetlights had just been turned on.

She said, "I think I swallowed a tooth." She retched, but nothing came up. "That's the fourth time. The papers?"

Charlie held the case for her to see.

She squinted at it and began to cry. "I'm going to have scars on my face."

Hooking the briefcase up over his wrist, Charlie took out his handkerchief and wiped the blood away from the little cuts around her eyes. "Never mind about that now." He folded the handkerchief over and dabbed at her mouth. "Who was that man?"

He walked her to the bench and helped her sit down. He could see without much trouble that she was nearly hysterical, so he let her crouch forward at the waist and cry. What to do? The nearest telephone was at Marlo's Fish and Steak House, a block beyond the tracks toward town. She needed a doctor, but he hated to leave her alone. When he looked down the road and then back in the direction of the lake, he couldn't see any cars. Even some kind of a hot-rod could take a message.

He felt silly, helpless, and a little afraid. That man on the train (or was he off the train now?), even though he hadn't looked too big, obviously meant business, funny business. And the woman—he looked her over. She was pushing forty, plump around the seams where her white blouse was pulled out and torn, a quivering fullness around her jowls. Her hair didn't have too much gray in it, and although it was wildly messed around now, he could see that it must have been neat and businesslike once. She had one arm around the briefcase on the bench, and she was gulping and wheezing as she bent over her knees.

He said, "It's going to be fine. We'll get you fixed up." Nervously he glanced down the tracks toward the freight cars. Couldn't see them any longer. And he couldn't see anyone in the huddle of dark against the sky lit by Bessemer converters. No getting around it, he didn't like this kind of stuff. One or both of these people had done something wrong, or they wouldn't have been smacking each other around. And it was no good getting tough with trouble. If you got tough, it got tougher. Just like the trains with their fat bellies full of smoke. Try to get the upper hand with them when you hadn't earned it, and they gave you one across the side of the head. Or rather, across the legs. He ran his fingers down his shinbones. No more hospitals. No, he'd get rid of her in a hurry.

It was 7:48, close enough to quitting time. But she was still letting her shoulders lurch from something bitter inside her. He patted her gently on the back, not wanting to touch her at all. He said, "Feel like walking now? We can get you to a phone, maybe call a doctor."

She jerked her head upright and peered at him, her eyes nearly swollen shut. "No! No time now. I've got to make a call, though, right away."

Her voice was harder than it had been, and he knew she was going to be all right. He was thankful. That meant less fussing and no blame to him. "Okay. We only got to go a block." Standing up, he locked the shanty door and put the warning sign flat on the ground behind the bench.

She said, "Thanks. Just get me to a phone." She paused and stood painfully, shifting from one foot to the other. "You won't be sorry."

"All right." Because her voice was angry, way underneath, Charlie was even happier about how things were going. You didn't have to worry about other people's anger, didn't have to get involved, as long as they weren't mad at you. Being hurt was something else, but angry too—that was fine. He didn't feel afraid.

They walked slowly together up the gravel riser to the sidewalk, and the streetlight, high and dim on a metal pole, made her look even dustier and more beat-up than before. He let himself feel very sorry for her. The briefcase, which she let dangle from one hand, kept bumping him in the leg and hurting, but when he tried to take it away from her, she yanked it back.

She said, "I'm holding it."

Her voice was frigid and husky, and he shut himself away from her after that. The leather case hit him in the leg again. Women didn't care if you got hurt.

She said, "God, my mouth aches."

He handed her his handkerchief, though he didn't know how that would help.

She pressed it against her jaw, opening and closing her mouth as if testing. "I suppose you wonder what goes on." She didn't look at him.

"No." He wanted to be all the way outside it now.

Suddenly she stopped, and the briefcase struck him in the kneecap. She said, "I left my purse on the train." Her eyes were horrified, blood-shot, held open as far as possible against the swelling.

Unwillingly, he said, "I can lend you a little maybe." He knew he should have expected this. It always managed to happen somehow.

She was talking to herself now, lisping only slightly in spite of the broken tooth. "Not the money. Don't need any." Starting to walk again, she twisted her ankle and leaned heavily against him. "But they'll know who I am. Of all the stupid—"

This wasn't the way it should be. Charlie felt interested in her, no matter how hard he tried to concentrate on the gray diamond-mesh hurricane fence around the soap factory to his right. Who was she talking about? Well, the man that hit her, certainly. And how many others? And who owned the briefcase? Glancing down at it as they passed another streetlight, he saw the initials, R. Q., gleaming on the flap.

To stop himself from wondering, he said the first thing that came into his head. "Are you a schoolteacher?"

"Of course not." She took a few more short steps, favoring her right ankle. "How much further is the phone?"

He pointed at the lit-up stucco building across the road and down a hundred feet. "That's Marlo's." He didn't want to know anything. He had to keep remembering that.

She said, "What is it?"

"A restaurant."

They started across the rough, pocked asphalt of the street toward the building, and for a few moments, Charlie had to concentrate on keeping them out of the weather holes.

She said, "Look, don't keep eating yourself up inside. I'm a reporter."

It didn't matter, and he didn't care. It probably wasn't true anyway. She didn't look like a reporter, and he'd be rid of her before long. They'd make the call, and the doctor would fix her up; then someone would come to get her. And he could go home to his room over the garage or maybe down to a movie and a glass of beer.

She said, "Really good of you to help. You might get yourself part of my bonus." She tried to smile at him, but he wasn't looking at her. "My name's Lily. What's yours?"

And because of that, because Lily didn't fit into R. Q. except perhaps in the middle that wasn't there, he knew that the leather case didn't belong to her. And he looked back over his shoulder beyond the string of streetlights at the crossing, expecting to see the man coming after his property. Now it was all wrong again, instead of all right. He'd helped steal a bunch of papers. Picked them up out of the ragweed for her.

She saw him glancing back. "Is anyone coming? No one could be coming, could they?"

Her voice was all unstrung again, and Charlie knew that she'd just remembered to worry about it. He'd get her to the phone, then fade out. You could get into more trouble with trains than anything else.

They stepped up over the low curb and headed for the narrow walk that led around the side of the restaurant. The hedge was in full leaf, seven feet high, and it ran along the length of the building and ended near the alley and some sheds. They came to the mouth of the walk.

She said, "Keep looking, will you? I can't see worth a damn."

But there was nothing to look at any more. The hedge was in the way. The restaurant had glass-brick panels on this side, but no windows. He couldn't tell whether many people were inside. Not many cars parked in front. Even so, he knew she'd hate to walk in front of anyone, looking like she did.

She said, "Is there a back door or something? I must be a mess."

Charlie nodded toward the walk between the hedge and the building. It was lit faintly by three yellow bulbs, spaced evenly to the cement area where the sheds and the rear door would be. He felt sorry for her now because she was so nervous. She kept the handkerchief either on her eyes or her mouth and tried to hurry. It was hard to keep in step with her, and he was glad she couldn't see that the handkerchief was dirty.

She tottered a little over a crack in the sidewalk. "Oh, if I ever get out of this one— How far is it to Chicago?"

"About a mile to the city limits."

"Is this still Indiana?"

It was getting harder to understand her. He saw that her lips were puffing up. "Yes."

They came to the end of the walk; two low sheds, painted dark green, stood a few yards apart back in the shadows where the light didn't reach well, and the smell of frying fish was heavy in the air. At least it was no hospital smell, nothing flowery and too clean. And it wasn't the smell of his room over the garage, musty like the powdered wood that puffed up between the floor-boards. It wasn't the smell of dry-rotted magazines. Funny how his nose had always haunted him, even when he'd been sure he wanted to marry some girl or other. He'd had to put his nose against their shoulders, against their necks to make certain. Like a dog. Well, almost. And the smells had never been right.

He and the woman stopped now by the three steps that led up to the back doorway. He knew there was a phone on a small landing to the right after you climbed the inside stairs.

He said, "Just go up the steps, and there's a phone booth around the corner." Maybe he could make this the end of it. She could do her own fretting. He knew a short-cut between the sheds to his room: just across the alley, then through a vacant lot, across the street, and up the garage stairs. She could do this herself. It was enough.

She turned and tried to look at him. "You've got to show me. I won't be able to see to dial."

"It's not a dial phone." He felt his thin wristbone shaking inside his shirt-cuff. If she'd go away now, it'd be all right.

"You've got to help me up the stairs. And what if someone saw me like this, by myself?"

She was pleading now, asking him to be sorry. He looked at a small electric fly-trap on a ledge against the back of the building. The wire grill sizzled with newcomers and the already dead. Below it was an eight-foot rectangular box, made of warped planks, with a slanting, hinged lid. The fishy smell was stronger, and it tortured his nose. He said, "Just hurry up and go in. I'll wait for you." He didn't think he would, really.

"Come on, you skinny jerk, help me. If you only knew how important this was." She shifted the briefcase to her other hand and dropped his handkerchief to the ground. It was a red one, so the blood didn't show, and he was just stooping over to pick it up when the man came around the edge of the building, the last yellow light behind him.

He was short and stocky with hanging shoulders and no hat, and he took a couple of steps toward them, limping. His pants were torn below the knee. Charlie knew who he was. No getting out now.

The man said, "Hello."

Charlie didn't straighten out of his crouch. From where he hunched, the man was just a silhouette, and he didn't want to see the face.

Clambering awkwardly up the steps, the woman started to cry, groping for the doorknob, but the short man caught her by the arm and hauled her back. She fell with a thump onto the cement, her legs twisting under her.

The short man said, "Shut up." He kicked her in the chest and picked up the briefcase.

Knowing with a kind of dumb sadness what would happen, Charlie stood up and lunged for the man. He felt his jaw and cheek explode before he could even touch the man's dark coat-sleeve, and he crumpled backwards, turning, to land chest down on his watch. He heard it break. Fuzzily, through one eye, he could still see what was going on, but he couldn't move. It was a relief. The worst of the trouble was probably done.

He saw the stocky man take out a blackjack and lean over the woman who was grunting and wheezing. He back-handed her hard on the temple. She didn't make any more noise. Everything stopped for a while, and Charlie tried to go to sleep. He looked with half an eye again and saw the big wooden box open beneath him, and then he was falling inside with a lot of bumpy things under-neath. Before the lid came down, the man hit him on the head.

The waiter was bald. Some kind of light shone from his scalp into Charlie's eyes, and then he woke all the way up. He could feel things moving under his shoulder blades. The waiter leaned the lid of the box against the wall and grabbed him by the vest.

The waiter said, "What's a gone on?"

His brain wouldn't work right, and everything hurt. He got one arm over the edge of the box and sat up, blinking at his hands.

"You try steal a lobsters, you get in a jail." The waiter was angry, and he reached across Charlie's chest and scraped him out of the box backwards.

Pulling up his legs in time to keep them from getting bumped, Charlie stumbled upright and felt his head. "Where's everybody?"

The waiter tapped him on the collarbone and waved his finger. "You dronk. Get out a here." His shirt was limp under his black coat, and his bow tie bobbed as he spoke.

Charlie watched the man's dark red face. "What happened to the woman?" Only after he said it did he remember that there had been a woman. Lying on the pavement, doubled up, groaning through her bruised lips. No, she'd been quiet at the end.

The waiter said, "No woman, no woman. But I'm get a cop pretty soon. Look a lobsters." He pointed.

Charlie looked. Inside the box crawled twenty or thirty big green ones, their antennae waving, their claws pegged with wood. On top, three were crushed on the head and back. Charlie felt worse, and his nose was pulsing with the sharp reek of the lobster smell. "I'm sorry."

The waiter shrugged. "Crazy." He paused and looked closely at Charlie. "You been in a fight? You mouth all hurt up on a side." He shut the lid of the bin.

Nodding, Charlie fingered his mouth and the back of his head.

"Should never a drink." The waiter's voice was softer. He reached into his pocket, rattling change. "Here's a half a buck. Go get a some food somewheres else. Not here."

Charlie took the money without thinking. "Didn't you see a man and a woman here a while ago? Short, square man. Woman all banged up."

"Nobody. Justa came out." He paused thoughtfully. "You knock her up?"

Everything was jumbled in Charlie's head, but he remembered the man who slashed sideways with a blackjack, and he remembered the briefcase. He looked around, his eyes feeling too big for his head. Nothing. Just his handkerchief, still there by the short stairway. He'd never pick that up. Her blood.

The waiter said, "You go. No trouble around here. Mr. Marlo get damn mad in a hurry."

Trying not to concentrate on anything, Charlie said, "Sorry about the lobsters. Can I pay you for them?" He didn't remember how much money he had.

The waiter waved him with the back of his hand. "Forget it. I use 'em a right now. Nobody know a difference."

Charlie started to walk. "Thanks."

"You go get a food. Okay?"

Charlie said, "Sure." But he wasn't sure at all. He walked away between the two sheds toward the alley, leaving the waiter behind. He went slowly, shuffling to keep from tripping over things, and got across the cinders of the alley and onto the path through the vacant lot without falling. The night was not chilly, but the wind that came over the frame-house roofs cut through his shirtsleeves and made his back cold where his vest was damp from the lobsters. Carefully, he recounted to himself what had happened: Lily, the telephone, the stocky man. It made only a small amount of sense. And he was all mixed up in it now.

He remembered quite clearly seeing the man kick the woman, then beat her over the head. Had she been killed? No, he wouldn't let his mind admit that. Bad enough without that kind of trouble. It was terrible to think of her being hurt badly again, after the beating-up she had taken only a few minutes earlier. Probably never been treated like that in her whole life.

He crossed a sidewalk, then the asphalt of a street, and came to his own walk that led back to the garage. He didn't feel particularly angry about being slugged himself. Secretly, he'd been expecting it all along. He'd asked for it by getting involved; but the woman, her eyelids, knees, and hands cut raw, hadn't deserved any more, even though she might have stolen some property. His head felt heavier than his feet, and both were hurting. He wanted a cup of coffee and some ice-cubes on his forehead before he could think, before he could decide whether he still had something to do.

The garage, behind his landlady's house, was brown brick, one and a half stories high, with a shallow sunporch twelve feet above the back yard. He wasn't supposed to use it, but soon the nights would be as hot as the days, and he knew he would. His door was on the side, and he navigated the stairway without turning on the light, because he knew he would have to use his hands on the deep steps, and he didn't want to see himself doing it. He got up to his room, switched on the lamp by the daybed, peeled off his shirt with the unbuttoned vest still on it, and went into the bathroom to kneel under the shower.

His neck chilled to whiteness and a towel draped over his shoulders, he listened to the water for coffee start to boil, and he began to think again, in spite of himself. Perhaps he should call the police. They'd find out whether anything had happened to the woman. They might be able to arrest the short man for assault. And in the process, everything about the briefcase might come to light. Well, that was all to the good. It should come out.

He heaped the fragments of his gold watch on the dresser and looked at them. Never be able to fix that right, and he couldn't afford a new one. He saw by his alarm clock that it was 9:58.

But what could he tell the police? A woman was pushed off a train. Who saw it? Evidently no one but him. They'd been on the last car, and the train had gone right ahead, and nobody'd been near the crossing. He and the woman hadn't met anyone on the street, and the waiter had seen nothing. Tell the police what? There's an unconscious woman with torn clothes and a bleeding face, and there's a man with a ripped pants leg who hurt his ankle jumping from the 7:36 to Chicago. They exist. They're somewhere. I saw them once, spoke to them. No evidence.

He spooned coffee into the open pan. On the shelf above the sink sat an old-fashioned cone-stack locomotive, a model in enameled brass. It had always been a favorite of his, and he looked at it now, trying to side-track his mind. Those would have been the days—when the fat, fast, snorting engines of today were still tea-kettles, less complicated. Now, all his choices melted into each other. Nothing was clear. The switches in a maze of tracks were freakish, either frozen or too loose. You never knew.

He remembered his six years on a section gang, his eleven as boss, then the eight years as a switchman, a cinder cruncher. Every buggy and every rail had been on his side, part of the hard game. Now he had to back off and warn the maniacs who didn't know any better than to drive in front of the Century or the Pennsylvania Limited.

He stirred the coffee and poured it into a cup, holding back the grounds with the edge of the spoon. He left the small kitchen, pulled down all the shades in his bed-sitting room, and put the cup on the arm of his overstuffed chair. Then he sat down, propping his feet carefully on a stool. For a moment, he felt as though he could stay out of it by just sitting, then going to bed after a while. He could keep quiet, tell no one, and maybe no blame would come to him. He stared at his wall calendar where the first days of June were checked off, but the tinted lithograph of freight cars above it brought back the old bogies: as watchman, he was supposed to report accidents, and this had been a kind of accident. But the railroad wouldn't be interested if no one filed a complaint, and he felt sure the woman wouldn't do that. It might never occur to her. Anyway, he wasn't sure she could. And the police in this town couldn't understand things very well. Chief Rakovitch could barely talk English. And Sergeant Dobryz-something-or-other always had the idea that whoever he saw first was the one to blame. Charlie remembered the time he'd listened to a crossing watchman testify after a police car had been side-swiped by a little Pennsylvania pop-buggy. No use. The Chicago police? Nothing had happened in Chicago. He felt he ought to be in the clear, but something kept saying no, and he couldn't figure out what it was.

He took the towel off his shoulders, tossed it into the bathroom, and put on a clean blue shirt. He looked at his face in the dresser mirror and saw the flesh tight over the cheekbones, pinched in at the temples, and now that he had washed the blood away from the corner of his mouth, there was only a slight puffing to show where he'd been hit.

It all came back to the briefcase. That's what had started the whole ruckus, caused the fight, and wound him up among the lobsters. Must be something in it that packed a wallop. If he could get hold of it, maybe he could find out who the woman was or who the stocky man was, or else find out who to get in touch with. But he didn't have any idea where it was now. He buttoned his shirt, put on his brown jacket. He'd have to go out to the tracks where the woman had been thrown off the train. If he found any of the papers from the briefcase, he'd try to do something. If not, then it was all finished as far as he was concerned. He combed back his dark, dangling hair and went down the stairs without turning off the lamp.

A half-moon was nearly overhead, but clouds were scudding high, thick, and fast, and it only lit the yard and the walk for a few seconds at a time. This trip, he didn't take the dark short-cut, but instead, walked down to the end of the block where a streetlight swayed in and out of the shadows from its own wires. There the houses ended. On the other side of the crossroad, a long strip of weed jungle and ditch lined the edge of the tracks, and the tracks themselves gleamed dully like a row of wave-crests on Lake Michigan beyond. He couldn't see the lake. The pumping station, the filtration plant, and a series of rock pilings shut it from sight. But he could hear it. He went down the long block toward his crossing.

The cool air didn't make his head feel better, and his legs jolted his body too much when he tried to hike his feet over each single track and each jutting board in the walk. He finally got to his shanty, feeling groggy and tired, and he unlocked the door and fished his flashlight out of the kindling box. Now, it all seemed stupid. He tested the light by shining it into the weeds. His eyes hurt. He decided he wouldn't look very carefully.

Hitching up his pants, he went along the same stretch of track he had followed to pick up the woman. As long as he kept on the ties outside the rail, he didn't need a light, but after the flat ground banked down to cinders at the edge, leaving him higher than the weeds, he became uncomfortable. Wasn't the best idea to be up in sight of everyone like this. He turned on the flashlight and slid cautiously down into the beginning of the high-sided ditch. Here he walked more slowly, stepping over tin cans, rusted spikes, and old tie-plates. Off to his left, above the looping tracks of the sidings, he could see the soap factory blowing steam and vapor up and away from him. He sniffed. The wind was still off the lake, so he couldn't get the deep, rank odor of the brewing fats.

Ahead, all was dark. The slightest dip from the ground level cut out the faraway streetlights and the lights from the factory, and the clouds were thicker now. He kept the flashlight at his feet, and he felt oddly overcareful and vulnerable. Because there was no semblance of a path, he had to walk next to the bank where the cinders ended and the weeds began. It was like trying to keep on a tightrope, and often he veered into the chest-high ragweed when his feet slipped.

After going sixty or seventy feet, he saw the twisted rims of the woman's glasses lying before him, and he knew this was the place. He turned the flashlight to all sides and began to hunt. Figuring to give himself about five minutes, he swept the light hastily along the embankment, then up to the rails. Nothing in sight. Next he tried the patches of weeds, nosing in and out of the squat clumps, bent over near the ground, and after he'd flipped over rain-soaked newspapers, ice-cream cartons, and the oldest of lunchbags, he found three slips of paper caught in the branched stems of a single large bush. They were more of the things that looked like pictures of checks, so he stuffed them into his pocket, knowing they were the real goods. He scouted around again and again, but found nothing else. He went back to where he'd seen her glasses rims.

He paused there, wondering what to do. His head was hurting more than before, and his legs felt punished all the way up into his backbone. Setting his jaw and preparing for the strain, he trundled himself up the bank to the blunt ties. One good look here and he'd call it quits. He knelt, then sat down on the rail to rest, remembering as he did so that this was the cardinal sin of all railroad men. No one ever stood or sat on a rail. But he was pooped. Running his light over the ties, inside and outside the bright rails, he spotted a brown corner of paper sticking from the far edge of a new tie. He leaned over to look. The mixture of dirt, slag, and cinders had been tamped down too far by some energetic section-hand, leaving a five-or six-inch cavity, and there, wedged in, was a thin paper parcel. He picked it up. Because it bent easily, was round, and had a hole in the middle, he guessed it must be a small record. He put the flashlight on the center and tore out a piece of the wrapping. He'd been right. A record, but no label.

Something made him snap off the light, and when he heard the noise, he knew it was for the second time. Someone was scuffing along the ditch from the west where the freight cars were still sided. Two of them. He could see their lights now and hear them muttering.

Putting the record into the pocket of his jacket, he let himself slide forward on the seat of his pants down the embankment. When he got to the bottom, he pushed himself upright with one hand, not caring about the way the cinders bit into his palm, and began walking back toward the shanty and the crossing. He wanted out of this. Someone had come to look for the rest of the papers. He was in no mood to offer them the back of his head again.

For a few moments, Charlie was glad he wasn't supposed to run, because he knew he'd be running and making noise if he could. His heart was yammering in his ears. They'd have heard him and caught him, and there'd have been forty new kinds of trouble. Then, without the help of the flashlight, he stumbled over a half-rotted keg of railroad spikes and fell down, the case of his light ringing loudly against one of the metal hoops.

He didn't bother to get up. Wouldn't do any good. So he crawled around the keg and into the wet, green jungle to his right and kept going. The grass roots sawed at his wrists, lagged at him, and he had to swipe at the forward weeds with his head to make even half a path.

Behind him, he heard the slither of men's shoes in the gravel; then their lights splayed into the weeds where he had gone. Because they didn't speak, he knew they were listening, and too late, he tried to freeze himself. They heard the noise of his scrabbling and came after him. Knowing he had no chance to get away, he dropped flat on the ground and hid his head in his arms. They could come and slug him. It didn't matter. He kept his eyes shut and tried to think of something else. No use trying to be any good when you couldn't run. People took advantage of you and chased you anyway. Before his legs had been so thoroughly broken by the humping freight car, no one had chased him for almost thirty years. Not since he was seventeen or eighteen and had been nearly caught lighting stink-bombs on Hallowe'en. But after the accident he'd been cornered and made to run in every dream.

He didn't want to cry, but he felt he was going to. He could hear the men nearby. It wouldn't be long. Maybe if he gave them the papers and the record, they'd let him go. Clutching at that, he sat up to fumble in his pockets. Then, he saw the lights were both past him, weaving and darting in the further clusters and up over the next rails. He sat still and hoped.

The lights either went out or went away. He sat for what seemed a long time, thinking that the men weren't so bright after all. He crawled a few feet to peek through to the next clump, but he couldn't see anything. Lying down again, he ran his nose into a low patch of skunk cabbage, and the little hood-like spathes rushed their foul smell back to the inside of his head and down his throat. He recoiled, shaking his shoulders and half-strangling, and scuffled, nose buried in his jacket, on his hands and knees without looking or caring.

He came to the first set of siding tracks before he knew it, and he stopped there, afraid he would sneeze or choke, looking around. It was not as dark as the other side of the weeds had been, and he could see the mercury-vapor lamps that strung the whole near edge of the soap factory. No one was in sight.

Either the men were waiting somewhere nearby, were gone, or had never existed. Maybe they'd been railroad men, detectives or inspectors, and he'd gotten into a lather over nothing. No, he knew how lazy they were, how most of their inspecting and policing was done over a bottle of beer or around a stove. None would get his shoes dirty in a weedy ditch unless he fell or was pushed. No, not inspectors. Two men had come looking for some scattered papers because a woman had sailed them off a train, and because a dumb crossing tender hadn't picked them all up at once.

He inched his way forward, heading for the lighted street, keeping himself away from the open rails. It took him ten minutes to go fifty yards, and when he came out into the last clearing and stood up to limp to the sidewalk that crossed the last tracks, his whole body was trembling, and he couldn't clench his fists or straighten out his fingers. He went down the walk, over the ruts in the road, and paused to lean against a lamp post. He had to stop. He felt it was silly to stand under the light, but he couldn't help it. If he didn't catch his breath now, he never would, and he'd have to sprawl in someone's yard on the way home.

When he opened his eyes and turned around to look, he knew what he would see. He wasn't even surprised. Coming through the brush next to the soap factory fence were two men, and they stopped at the sidewalk on the other side of the street and looked at him. They both had on dark suits, without hats, and one was short and stocky. They looked at each other. The short one nodded.

Charlie began to run without knowing he could run, and his legs burned outward through his pants till he expected to see the bones shredding in splinters. He went right for the nearest house, across the side yard, and into the shadow of the garage. Here the lights were all shut off again. He lurched through a flower garden, dim and knee-high, through a scrubby hedge, and around the corner of the next garage. His eyes wouldn't work any more.

Groping wildly with his hands, he felt for the side of the garage, then followed it to the alley and turned right along the palings of a fence. His legs wouldn't stay straight, kept buckling at the knees, and when he stopped and rubbed them with his hands, he found he was shin-deep in a pile of newly cut grass that had been dumped outside the yard. Without thinking, he dropped himself into it with his back against the fence and began to cover his legs, his body, and finally his head. He slid his arms forward then, hoping they would be under it too, and waited.

The men came by from somewhere. He could hear them mumbling, and one of them said the word "watchman." Breathing softly through his mouth and trying to keep the tickling of the grass out of his nose, he lay still. He couldn't see any lights. Probably afraid to use them around houses. The voices went away, and he pretended, counting to a hundred twice, that his legs didn't belong to him.

Well, they knew who he was, and that made it worse. Couldn't ignore them now or make believe nothing had happened. Some kind of bugs were crawling around in the cut grass, chirping. He lifted his head, shook it, and leaned back against the wooden palings, wondering whether they knew his name or where he lived. Wasn't an easy thing for them to find out right away. He didn't have many friends. Maybe it would be safer, though, to sleep somewhere else for the night, until he could find out what the papers and the record meant. His Aunt Myra in South Chicago might put him up.

By blinking his eyes and squinting through the dark, he could see across the alley and between two houses to his own street. Wasn't far. And he'd need to get some of his money out of the coffee can before he went anywhere else, even for a night. He listened as hard as he could. Only the faint honking of cars on the distant boulevard to Chicago. And the crickets or whatever.

He stood up, pulling himself hand over hand by the nearest paling, and he didn't feel particularly afraid. Just kind of sick. The worst he could get would be a beating, and he realized, in a way, that a beating would make everything much simpler. He went across the alley, not even wishing he could tip-toe, and made straight for his street. He kept his eyes aimed between the two one-story houses that helped to prop him from time to time, and when he came out of their shadows and stumbled over the sidewalk and into the narrow street, he aimed his eyes again: this time at his landlady's house, only fifty feet further to the right. He angled off toward it and kept his legs working somehow. At the turn of the narrow walk back to the garage, he let his eyes wander for a moment down to the end of the block, and he saw the two men there beyond the streetlight. They had already begun to run toward him, but he didn't hurry. He didn't even pause at the side door of the big front house, because he knew his landlady was a bit skittish, and she wouldn't let him use the telephone at this time of night. Especially not to call the police and cause commotion. He walked to his garage door, opened it, stepped inside, turned on the stair light, and got up the stairs by holding both hands against the walls, his arms stiff.

He turned out the lamp by the daybed because he didn't need it, and he felt for the coffee can in the bottom of the magazine rack. He took out the forty-six dollar bills and put them in his pants pocket. It wouldn't take much longer.

The door at the foot of the stairs rattled quietly, and Charlie opened the window that led to the little sunporch and sat on the sill. He heard one of the men whisper and the latch click shut. He slid his feet out on the tarred surface of the porch, keeping his head inside the window. When he heard two kinds of shuffling on the steps, he turned and went to the low railing; he stepped over it, crouched, and sat on the spouting, then twisted his body from the waist up, held the spouting with his hands, and let himself dangle. He relaxed his fingers, kept his legs limp. The cement pavement had only been six feet from his shoes, and he made himself collapse as he landed. He cracked his elbow and his upper arm, but his legs didn't hurt any more than they had before.

Getting up, he limped carefully across the yard into the neighbor's zinnia beds. As far as he could see, it was blessedly dark, a tangle of trees and shrubs, back porches. He wouldn't walk on any sidewalks, on any streets. Just straight down for two blocks, through a sunken vacant lot, and there would be the boulevard. And he could catch a bus for South Chicago and Aunt Myra. Maybe he could sleep on the bus. He circled a bulky flower bush, feeling a little drunk, and he wondered how long it would take him to be afraid again. Not long.

CHAPTER TWO

Taking a deep breath, Cooper nudged the other man ahead of him into the office and held the briefcase across his chest with both hands as though it were bullet-proof.

The man at the desk looked up, looked at his watch, looked at the ceiling, and said, "Where've you been?"

"Your name Hindruth?"

"Yes. Why weren't you here last night?"

Cooper fidgeted. "My name's Cooper. This is Praksar, Milan Praksar." He nodded at the other man.

"Did you bring the documents?"

"Yeah." He looked at Hindruth's face, squinted and looked hard.

"Well, how's the Senator?"

It would be all right. "Okay, I guess." Because Hindruth was little and didn't look tough, Cooper felt better. The man's eyes, if any color at all, were just barely blue, and his wavy gray hair was thin enough to show patches of scalp. "We had a little trouble."

Hindruth shifted in his seat. "Trouble? Not much, I hope. That's one thing we have to avoid."

The office was hot, and the walls were painted a runny green. Through a doorway beyond the desk, Cooper could see another john-sized room with composition flooring and dustless squares where pictures had hung. A filing cabinet and a straight chair stood beside the desk, and nothing else. The heat rolled around.

Cooper said, "It may be a real headache. I don't know."

Praksar said, "It ain't a headache. It's a pain in the ass." He started to laugh, leaning against the outer door, but he choked it off.

Frowning, Cooper looked at the wide cheekbones and mouth, the crew-cut hair, and the lean, powerful build of Praksar. The genius. "Don't pay no attention to him, Mr. Hindruth. He don't have to think."

Hindruth pointed at the chair beside the desk and opened his cigarette case. "Let's hear it."

Squirming gently, Cooper tried to get his backsides to fit in the hard angles of the chair. He stared at the bright windows. "I got the briefcase okay." He patted it. "But between Gary and the city limits we had an unfortunate incident." He glanced at the older man and felt uneasy. His hands began to sweat, and he hid them behind the briefcase. It was silly. What could happen?

Hindruth said, "Well?"

Cooper cleared his throat and shrugged. "We had the observation car all to ourselves, except for this woman. The train wasn't crowded, and a lot of people were in the diner up ahead of us. Neither me nor Praksar had seen her before on the train. She might've been there, but she didn't look like much, so maybe we just didn't notice. Well, we were just relaxing there, thinking of nothing, and she come up to us and started jawing away about her losing her money or something, and I was reaching into my pants to hand her a buck to get rid of her. But then she leaned over and snatched the briefcase right out of my lap and ran for the diner."

Hindruth said, "Why didn't you have it locked to your wrist, for God's sake?" His face, pink before, had gone white.

Cooper let his voice get a little higher. "I know, I know. But I didn't. Well, the dumb Slovak here kept sitting like he was watching a movie or something, but I went after her and caught her between the cars. I still thought, see, maybe she was trying to swipe some money, and so I didn't get too rough. But she had half the outside door open before I could stop her. She kept saying how she was going to throw the case away if I didn't leave her alone. Of course, I saw she was wise to something then. I tried to grab it away from her, but she jumped right out of the train. So help me, jumped right out, and the train was going so slow, she didn't break her neck. I saw the case flop open and some of the stuff go flying all over the place." He remembered the broken glasses and the blood running down from her eyes. Maybe if he'd tried talking instead of hitting...

Hindruth stood up. "You mean you didn't even have it locked? You didn't even lock the thing?"

Waving his plump hand from side to side, Cooper looked at the desk top. "I realize that. It was dumb. But I'm not used to being fooled with. It was a big surprise."

Hindruth sat down. "Jesus!"

Cooper hurried on. "At first I didn't know what to do. Some guy from the crossing back a ways was coming to help her, and when I decided to jump off too, there wasn't any room. We were smack up against some freights. Praksar, the brain, came out on the platform then, and I told him to get off at Englewood and take a cab back. Then we came to the end of the freights and I hopped off, but the train was going faster, and I damn near broke my ankle." Unable to think of some right words, he saw in his mind the dark, the weeds, and three nuts limping nearer and nearer each other. Well, it hadn't been such a hot night's work.

The traffic on Wabash four floors below suddenly made more noise, and the brilliant glass of the window shook a little. Cooper felt himself shaking with it, felt himself nodding, and he frowned.

Hindruth said, "I don't like this story very much so far."

Cooper looked down at his own pants where they were crinkled like cardboard reinforcement in the crotch. "You think I like it? Well, it was getting real dark by then, and I had a hell of a time walking at first. Took me a long time to get to the nearest crossing where there was a light. But I found them, her and this guy from the crossing. I caught up, running on the bum ankle, beaned them both, and got the briefcase. Nobody saw me. I don't think so." Two scared-white faces and the smell of fish. A skinny guy with black hair who swung his arm around so slowly you could count the creases on his knuckles where his fist was only half-clenched. A real nut.

Hindruth said, "I hope you don't think that's the end. Come on, what happened?"

Cooper pulled his mind together, feeling sorry for himself. He should have written it all down so he could mail it like a report. You could get all tangled up talking because you had to think at the same time. And thinking was always messy.

Hindruth said, "What's the matter with him?"

Praksar smiled, and his deep eyes disappeared behind his cheeks. "He's sleepy. We had a night."

Cooper spoke loudly. "Shut up!" It was bad enough handling one struggle. "No, that ain't all. I thought it was, maybe. You see, I knew she'd wanted the stuff bad, and they had time, while I was getting my pants about tore off me, to pick up what was spilled. I figured she wanted all of it, like me. And I had to go stand back at that crossing, or Praksar wouldn't ever have found me. Took him fifty-five minutes to get back. The sap took time to hire a car. While I was standing there, I couldn't check the brief-case. Not enough light, and besides, it would have been kind of funny-looking. I didn't want to walk back along the tracks either. Wouldn't do much good in the dark. Finally, Praksar came, we drove to a bar, checked the stuff with a list I got, and some was missing."

Hindruth's voice was quiet. No unhappiness showed yet. "Then you went back to the place where she jumped out?"

"Yeah. We got a couple flashlights at a drugstore and hiked back there. We found some of the stuff near those freight cars I told you about, but then another guy came along. He shined his light on something he picked up, and we chased him all over the place. Finally we saw him out in the light. It was the same guy as before, the crossing guy." He paused. "Well, to tell the truth, he ducked us."

Two pigeons flapped past the window without looking, and Hindruth put his hands flat on the desk as though bracing himself. "What's missing from the briefcase?"

"A record and three check photostats."

"Important?"

"Kind of. Well, yes." Cooper scratched his ear and waited. The other could ask the questions now. That was easier. The story could just sit there between them for what it was.

"Could some of it be lying where it first fell?"

Cooper shook his head. "Me and Praksar went back and looked for another hour or more. Nothing."

"What about the woman? Where is she?"

Cooper shrugged. "Didn't see her again."

"Maybe she's got some of the papers, not this crossing man." Hindruth rocked forward in his desk chair.

His face was intent, but Cooper could see the weakness in it, the lack of know-how, and he felt stronger. He pursed his lips, making them bulge out fat till he could see them by looking down his nose. "No. I frisked her when I got the case back."

"What's the crossing man's name?"

"Charles Bell." A slight mistake. In his mind Cooper snapped his fingers four or five times, hoping for something, anything to say quick. It came. "It was on his door-buzzer."

There was a dead pause. Hindruth said, "How did you know where he lived?"

"Oh, we asked somebody." It was going to get by. Relaxed, he watched the tension fade away.

Hindruth brushed off the front of his damp shirt. "I'm sure the Senator will be overjoyed when I tell him this. Did you get a line on Bell?"

"How could I?" No, not the Senator. He wouldn't come into it, not yet. He always scattered blame around like handbills. They'd have to make a shush on their own, and that was perfect.

Hindruth said, "So now we have to worry about him."

For the first time Cooper allowed his voice to get gruff. "If he takes what he's got to any one of the three bad newspapers in this town, we can all go home and hide." He stared at Hindruth. "I figure it this way. That woman probably works for a paper hereabouts and—"

"Then why don't we find her?"

Cooper tapped on the briefcase for emphasis. "We got to plan that he didn't give them to her. Our only chance. We got to worry about keeping him away from those news-rags."

"Maybe so. But where is he?"

"I don't know." I don't know, and the steep stairs to the second floor of the garage, if only the face that looked so dumb was dumb enough to come back and get afraid. "But if the cops get him, we're all right. Any cops around here. Even them in that suburb. I mean, you can work a fix, can't you?"

Hindruth cocked his head. "What? What makes you think the police want him?"

Knowing he was going to stammer, Cooper said, "No reason. Just *if*. He looks like the kind that gets in trouble easy."

"You mean like you? Listen, if the newspapers see any of that—Which record was it?"

"The Corrigan one."

"Oh, God! Well, if the papers get it, our stink will be just a little stink next to the great big stink." Hindruth got up and walked around to the front of the desk. "You know whose fault that'll be?"

"Yeah, yeah. It won't happen though." He was not impressed by Hindruth. The man's featureless, good-natured face couldn't scare a ten-year-old, and that was the only piece of luck so far. If he'd been someone like Quiller— "Look, it's this way: I've figured out this guy's psychology."

"Talk about something you can spell."

"I mean—"

Hindruth said, "Mr. Cooper, this is going to be your baby. I'm going to have lots of other things to do." He took the briefcase. "I'll expect you and what's-his-name here to handle it. And God help you if you let the bottom fall out of everything. Convention time is sooner than anybody seems to think."

Cooper nodded. "Sure. I was going to take care of it anyway. Just thought you ought to know. I'm responsible for the damn things, all of them."

Undoing the catch of the briefcase, Hindruth said, "That's settled then. In the meantime, I have to go on as if nothing had happened." He paused and looked at his wristwatch. "You can get out of here now."

And Cooper looked at the electric clock on the floor by the filing cabinet where a small pile of dust and flaked plaster had been swept together, then stepped on several times. It was nearly eleven. "Okay, but I'll need more dough." He stood up, not believing, as Hindruth reluctantly put two fifties into his hand. "I said some dough. I can't do much on this."

Hindruth's face was flushed. "That's all for now. Come back when it's gone."

Cooper waved the two bills at Praksar. "This is money, see?"

Coming away from the door, Praksar took his hands out of his pockets and buttoned his dark, too-heavy suit-coat. "We gettin' a run-around?"

"Get out of here." Hindruth was almost squeaking. "You've botched things up enough for one day."

"That's that, huh?"

"Yes."

Cooper put his hand on Praksar's lean, hard chest and jogged him toward the door. "All right, I might have known. I'll call you in a couple hours."

"Don't bother."

"Won't be no trouble at all. You'll want to see us." And he shouldn't have said it, but he let the words hang back there in the office as he got Praksar out ahead of him.

Down the elevator and out onto the sidewalk, he thought of five better ways to have said everything, but what the hell. The buildings and the Elevated shadowed the street completely, but the dust in the air was flashing anyway, and it churned up over the short restaurant awnings. The dirt in the briefcase would fill Hindruth's mind, and he wouldn't be able to think of anything else carefully.

Praksar lagged behind to stare over his shoulder at the hips of a passing woman, and Cooper had to grab his arm and steer him around the corner onto Randolph. Nothing would be a cinch. He let his mind riffle through the contents of the briefcase, remembering photographs like French postcards, affidavits, check and ledger photostats, all the best kind of blackmail. He kept reminding himself that last night he had played no more for keeps than the Senator was doing, than Hindruth would have to do. They had to cover him.

They passed the side of Marshall Field's, and the sudden entrance into sunlight at the corner of State Street dizzied him for a moment. He stopped by a newsstand and made Praksar stop too. A truck swung by and dropped a bundle of the early-afternoon edition of an evening newspaper on the curb. The newsy, an old man, gaunt, wizened, with a drinker's nose and complexion, snapped the thin wire around the bundle and lifted the papers, a few at a time, to the metal shelf of his stand. Cooper bought a paper.

And Charles Bell was walking around with a recording and three photostats in his pocket, maybe. He hoped so. He'd seen too often the kind whose only thought at first was to cut and run. Bell had to be that kind. Had to be. Even if only for a day.

Praksar said, "We gonna stand here, for Chrissakes?"

Glancing down the front page of the paper, Cooper let his eye skim a story about a presidential candidate's latest statement from a New York hotel and another story about a huge air-conditioning system being installed at the convention hall in the midst of the stockyards.

It was there at the bottom, and staring hard and reading fast, with a kind of relief and no visible surprise, he found that the dead body of an unidentified woman had been discovered in a garage apartment in an Indiana suburb, and that the woman had been badly beaten around the head, and that the police were interested in interviewing Charles Bell, a crossing watchman, who lived in that apartment and whose present whereabouts was unknown.

CHAPTER THREE

When the water began dripping on his face, Charlie woke up. Above him, through the half-lit darkness, he could see the rust-eaten rainspout along the edge of a roof and a strip of sky. Where was he? He started to turn over and rammed his elbow and knee into the side of a wooden building. Brushing his hand across his face, he sat up and looked at the small garage beside him, then at the short back yard between him and the house. Aunt Myra. He remembered losing his nerve after the bus ride, being unable to ring her doorbell, unable to think of anything to say to her. Well. He ducked when more water trickled down, and he shivered.

It was dawn, and he'd have to start for work. But as he tried to stand up and felt the throbbing in his legs, he knew it was no use. Might as well forget about work today. He tried to remember whether he'd ever intended to go back to the crossing and stand there again with the warning sign and listen to the noise of the engines. Probably not.

He felt himself going to sleep with his back against the garage. No. She'd wake up in the house and see him, come out and get him, ask questions and be nice. He hadn't seen her since before his accident, and he didn't want to now.

He crawled carefully along the side of the garage till he came to the door. Then, pulling himself up by the knob, he looked inside. No car. Maybe left it in the street in warm weather. He let himself in, closed the door, and curled up beside a kerosene can and a box of kindling, wishing they were on fire. He needed to sleep. But his mind didn't run away quickly enough because he suddenly remembered the men who'd chased him. Hadn't seen them after he'd got on the bus. Hadn't seen the woman, Lily, either. Beneath his arms, in his jacket pockets, he could feel and hear the paper, feel the outline of the record. Everything was the same. Not good, but at least the same. He didn't have to think right away. Not for a while. While his legs pulsed evenly, always a fraction of time behind his heartbeats, he went to sleep again.

Birds were wrangling outside the window, and he listened to them for a while before he sat up. His jacket came away from the cement floor reluctantly, leaving some of its fuzz in a patch of car grease. He felt rested and dirty, no longer cold, and he knew he'd slept an impossibly long time because his eyes weren't the least bit stuck together.

Hauling up his pants legs beyond his knees, he looked at his shins. They were splotchy and inflamed, and several of the long scars were more purple than they'd been before. He felt them, making sure the pain wasn't in any one spot. Good enough to walk on. Maybe he'd see a doctor in a few days.

He put one hand on the windowsill to pull himself up and remembered the men again, how they had come up his stairway, how they'd kept popping up out of the night, trying to get him, to touch him. He looked at his thin, dark work pants and felt his hand begin to tremble against the sill. His blue shirt was stiff with sweat under the arms, and he was going to be afraid. No. He couldn't go back to his rooms now. He felt he could never go back, not unless he had a lot of people with him. Well, where could he go? He took his hand away from the window and retied the loosened laces of his high safety shoes. His mind wouldn't work.

When he finally stood up, he stared through the window and over the tile or shingle roofs and the crouching trees, and he saw the maze of wires that meant the IC electric trains. Why did he have to do anything at all? Easy to say the hell with Lily or whatever her real name was; easy to say the hell with the men who chased him. He could stay in South Chicago, get a job, then maybe in a couple weeks go back to his place and pick up his things. But still he felt unsure.

And he felt hungry, but he knew he wouldn't go knock on the back door and sponge something from Aunt Myra. Wouldn't do any good to start talking to her again. She was always after him to marry somebody. Anybody. But there were some things you just couldn't have. A woman, for instance. Wouldn't be many more years before his body would quit aching. You had to change if you wanted a woman, and he couldn't change what he was. He'd always liked getting dirty at his job. A good feeling. And years ago, there'd even been one girl who'd liked it too, rubbing the grease off his pants and making herself a beard of it. What was her name? No more dates. Well, it didn't matter, really. There were other things, like beer. With his eyes nearly shut, he glanced around the sunlit back yard. It was late, probably after noon, and the air was dull gold and close. Time to go. There was no sign of anyone moving on the back porch or through the kitchen windows.

He went out the small garage door and turned onto the narrow sidewalk toward the alley, keeping his head down as though expecting to be hit.

Aunt Myra's voice came from behind him. "Is that you, Charles?"

He kept walking. You could never be unseen when you wanted to.

She said, "Just a minute, son."

He felt silly. She'd always called him that, even though she was only ten years older than he was, and his mother had been so small, so silent. Way long ago.

She said something else, but without turning to look at her, he went sauntering carelessly past the garage and into the alley, pretending he could pick up his feet if he wanted to. He angled right and headed toward the mouth of the alley which would bring him out near the corner of 77th and Exchange. Because of the heat, he took off his jacket, held it under his arm, and felt in his pants pocket to make sure the money was still there. The sun burned through the branches and the telephone wires. It wasn't going to be easy to know what to do, because he'd gotten off the track last night, far off, and every possible move was strange to him. He'd be reported today, certainly, for not being on the job. Maybe someone would get killed at his crossing with him not there, but he shut that out of his mind. Well, it meant he had no job. That was the place to start. No job? Then no sense going home. Especially since he didn't know where the men might be.

Feeling he'd settled at least one thing, Charlie walked across the street toward the slightly raised platform of the IC Station. The two sets of tracks that went down the middle of diagonal Exchange reminded him too much of his own wide bunch of rails, so he didn't look at them. He went up the shallow stairs to the enclosed ticket office. From here, he could go all the way downtown to Randolph Street or back in the other direction to 91st. He couldn't make up his mind. The Loop would be too hot, too hustled, and there was nothing at 91st except Mexicans and the end of the line. He went around the corner of the narrow corridor to face the ticket window, but no one was behind it. Late lunch or something. He limped out onto the platform and sat on a bench beside a peanut machine. That left it up to nobody. He'd take the first train in either direction.

It was good to sit in the shade, but he still couldn't think the way he wanted to. A car went by occasionally on Exchange or turned and bumped over the tracks. A man came out of the drugstore and yawned. The platform was hot. Well, he'd get a job first, then think. Couldn't be anything hard, maybe night watchman in a warehouse or a janitor or just sweeping. No need to be proud. He was out of the habit. An easy job, a place to stay, then begin to think. He settled back on the bench, feeling better.

The first train came from the direction of Chicago, swaying along the rails, its wiry superstructure spitting sparks against the high power lines. The crossing gates went down, and the bells rang. He stood up, far from the edge of the platform, and waited till the train was at a full stop. Then he went through one of the sliding doors and sat in a wicker seat, facing front. He tried not to hear the whining throb of the electric motors nor smell the miasma of dead perfume and cigars. It was no use. The motors stirred up a knot of fright in his stomach, just as steam engines always did. He got a window up about six inches and sat, his jacket across his lap, waiting for the street to move.

Only two other people were in the car: a fat, middle-aged woman and a young Mexican boy with wavy hair. The train hummed into a crawl, then went faster, and Charlie paid a staggering conductor his fare to 91st. The cooler air felt good, and he watched the houses scatter till they gave way to a flat area of weedy cinders where the small coal yards and junk piles began. He picked up a discarded Chicago newspaper from the seat opposite him and started to read.

The paper had been folded inside out, so he read the comics first, then the sports page. Saving the want ads for last, he turned to the front page. He had glanced at nearly everything else before he finally came to the story at the bottom of the page. Then, for several minutes, he couldn't make out what he was reading. He kept seeing his own name, and he didn't believe it; it didn't seem real.

The only fact he could get into his head at first was that Lily was dead. It didn't actually make him sad. More a kind of relief. Then, with a splash of light inside, his mind woke up, and he saw that she'd been found in his apartment. The police were looking for him. The train rattled and swayed and he sat there, his mind racing ahead of it, down some other tracks to a crossing, and he remembered the men at his door. They'd killed her and put her in his room, and now he'd have to do all kinds of things he didn't understand, couldn't do.

He didn't know the train had stopped until he heard the conductor shout. It was the end of the line, 91st Street. His brain numb, his legs clumsy under him, he went out onto the bright platform, wanting to hold up his jacket and hide his head in it. Only a few people shoved by him and clicked their shoes on the uneven boards, and he stood there, wavering, not knowing what to do. All he was certain of was that he had no use for 91st Street. It didn't mean anything now. Couldn't try to get a job. Without reading the story in the paper again, he crumpled it and threw it down between the tracks. A quiver of pity made his throat jerk, nearly made him gag, and he swallowed hard to fight it. He hadn't done anything. How could you get into so much trouble without doing anything? He'd always tried to be good, had helped people once in a while.

A train crept up on the other side of the platform, heading back toward town, and when the doors opened, he got in and sat way to the rear, hunching down in the close, hot air. The news story hadn't described him, just gave his name; but he felt huge and conspicuous, even though he could look down and see how narrow he was. Nothing made sense. All last night and today, he'd been walking around underwater, in the dark. Nothing to think of or at, and still nothing. He sat for a long time, feeling the perspiration blotching his shirt. The train didn't move. He felt all the way outside of everything, frightened, and he couldn't tell anyone why. No one could tell him.

The burring noise of the electric motors grew louder, began to whinny, and the train started. He felt sick and feverish, but he wasn't angry. He didn't know anyone well enough to be angry with. The men? He didn't know who they were or what. He pressed his knuckles under his nose to hold away the smell of his own fear.

He was on the side away from the sun, and after a few moments when the conductor came, he wished there were even more shadows. It didn't matter. The man's wrinkled white face kept its bored expression, then went away. Staring through the dust-flecked window at the litter in the fields and around the unpainted houses, he was suddenly sure of one thing: he didn't want to go to the police. They wouldn't believe anything he told them. He'd put his foot in it all the way along. And he wanted to open the window and throw out the record and the pictures of checks, put them back where they belonged: in the weeds beside railroad tracks. He felt the record in his jacket pocket, bending it against his knee, and the idea came.

Maybe what the record said would be evidence. It belonged to the man who owned the briefcase, R. Q., and maybe it would say who he was, get him involved. He could take that to the police, and it might mean something. But he had to be sure. If he went now and told them the story and they played the record to see if it helped, it might be hillbilly music or something, and then he'd be done for. The pictures of checks didn't look like they meant anything, but the record might. He stared out the window again, trying to think.

The train had turned slightly to the left and was yawing and squeaking down the middle of Exchange. Each time they stopped at a little station, Charlie kept his eyes away from the people getting on and off or standing beside the benches on the platforms. His car was more than half full, and one old man, with hairs growing from his ears, lowered himself into a seat nearby. The pint of whisky in the man's back pocket was tipping out, ready to fall into the aisle. Charlie didn't look at it. Couldn't think of that.

He watched the lane of the street on his side flow past the low brick stores and taverns, and then they came to the wide intersection at 71st Street. Off to his right, the South Shore Country Club gate hunched like the stucco-arch entrance to a fun house. The traffic was heavy, turning by it toward the Outer Drive. The train angled left again and went down the broad middle of 71st, and Charlie stood up, easing his legs from between the seats, and leaned against the edge of the door. At the far end of the car, the conductor poked his head in and muttered, "Bryn Mawr." The train slowed and stopped.

Once outside, he didn't pause to give his legs a chance to hurt. Keeping his head down, eyes on his feet, he steered through the standing groups of people, through the covered end of the station, and down the steps to the edge of the tracks. He waited till the train pulled out again, waited for the cars and taxis to go away, then crossed half the street to the north curb. Had to find out about this as soon as he could, had to do something. He walked along the store-fronts, keeping next to the glass and away from people, and the sun lashed down out of the wires and dust until his shirt was wet everywhere. A record shop. There would have to be one nearby. As he passed a newsstand, he wanted to buy a paper, but he knew it would be the same edition he'd seen on the train. That could wait a couple of hours.

He went down to the second block, looking from the corners of his eyes at each store window, and his kneecaps began to feel like ripe tomatoes. He'd have to sit down again soon. Having just made up his mind to go into the next bar for a glass of beer, he saw the record shop. It was small and lined, up and down and over the top, with glass bricks. With his shoulder against the bricks, he stared at the window display. A placard leaned on a short pyramid of record albums, and he looked at the picture of a man in tight pants, yowling up at a balcony full of women. The colors all ran together, dripping purple and black down toward the man's wide-open mouth. Charlie felt his own mouth, then his lips and cheeks. He hadn't shaved since early yesterday, and his hair was loose and stringy. He wouldn't look like much, but he'd have to try it anyway. He went inside, shutting the door as quietly as he could, working in his mind for the right way to say things.

The muffled hubbub of music struck him, and he stood by the door and tried to find himself. The walls of the small shop were bare, except for a single line of colored pictures halfway around. They were more singers and things like that, and he only gave them a glance. A woman stood behind a counter at the rear, and behind her were dozens of high shelves stacked with green-jacketed records. At the side was something that looked like a telephone booth with young girls bulging from the door, and the music came from there, a lot of violins. Because one of the young girls was talking to the woman behind the counter, he hung back, fingering the outline of the record and shifting from leg to leg.

The woman who ran the shop had on a canary-colored blouse with no sleeves, and her thin, pointed nose was shiny with the heat. Her light hair was all swept up, frizzled on the top. She said, "That's all the Debussy we have. You girls are getting too sophisticated."

Charlie looked at the girl, then at the other girls in the booth. They all looked alike, but were different sizes. The one at the counter was fat and flat-chested; her calves were large and went straight down into her socks, like posts. White blouses, bright skirts, and all chattering louder than the music.

The fat girl said, "Well, have you got any Benjamin Britten? Or Walton?" Her voice was shrill.

The woman said, "I guess so. I'll dig them out." She turned to the shelves. "I wish you girls would stick to one thing. I just laid in a stock of populars."

The fat girl looked back toward the booth and laughed. "Oh, that stuff."

A thin, nervous blonde at the edge of the small crowd laughed too and made a face. "Such corn." She closed her eyes, listening to the violins swoop, nodding behind the slow rhythm.

Charlie thought of going to a different shop, but his legs were so tired he didn't want to. Bracing himself inside, he went up to the counter and propped one elbow on it.

The woman put down four records in colored cardboard envelopes in front of the fat girl. "This is it." The fat girl began to look at them.

Turning to Charlie, the woman said, "What can I do for you?"

He drummed his fingers on the counter and tried to look musical. "I'd like to hear some records." He couldn't remember the names of any.

The woman smiled and raised her very thin eyebrows. "Which ones?"

Desperately, he looked over her shoulder and pointed to the smallest one he could see. It had a picture of people dancing on a drum. "Well, that one." He waved his hand vaguely. "And the one next to it."

The woman looked puzzled. She pulled out the two records that had been protruding out of line and turned them so he could see better. "These?"

Charlie nodded and pursed his lips. They were larger than the record he had, but not by too much. Probably the same machine would work them all. He took them from her and pretended to look carefully at the labels.

She said, "The Boston Symphony does a good job."

The fat girl leaned over and peeked, then glanced up at Charlie. "Mendelssohn." She let her lower lip hang down to give a small raspberries.

He turned the records so she couldn't see. He frowned as though he were considering thoughtfully. If he could get these into the booth and shut the door, he could play his record and see what it was. But there were so many girls around. He could smell the steam that rose from the perfume on their shoulders and the soft stickiness of their hands. If they'd go away, everything would be all right. He said, "Could I listen to these?"

The woman looked toward the booth. "You'll have to wait a few minutes. The player is being used."

The fat girl let out a little squeal and waved a record in the air. "*Façade*." She said it two or three times, and several of the girls ran to her side to look. Then they all came. The last one shut off the violins and brought the record with her.

Charlie edged toward the booth. They were grouped around the fat girl now, listening to her talk, hum, and giggle, and he stepped inside the small cubicle, closing the door quietly. It was lined with cream-colored plasterboard that had thousands of tiny holes in it, and on the shelf at one side was a machine with a fuzzy turntable. He put his jacket on the single stool and, with his back to the glass of the door, pulled the record from his pocket. Hotter than a steam bath, the booth nearly made him sick. He tore the brown paper away from the record and looked at it. It was a few inches smaller than the others, but when he tried it on the turntable, the hole in the middle was large enough. He picked up the needle arm and looked for a switch, but the machine started to turn by itself. He put the needle down on the edge and listened hard.

When he heard the high babbling from outside the booth, he glanced over his shoulder and saw the girls staring through the glass at him. They were frowning and talking among themselves, and the fat girl pushed to the front, looking red and angry. He turned away. If they'd only give him a couple minutes. Then the record started to make noise.

It began with a low gruffle and changed to a yawning squawk; then came a few short clicks of different pitch. It kept that up with variations. He took the record off and looked at it. He recognized the sounds: just like when his mother's victrola used to need winding. The record looked all right, was cut on both sides, not scratched to speak of, and he began to damn his luck because the machine was probably broken. It was suddenly too hot, too sweet in the booth, and, stuffing the record back into its paper cover, he picked up his jacket and the other records and opened the door.

The fat girl said, "Talk about squeezing in ahead."

As he hurried between them, another girl looked him up and down and said, "Should we disinfect the place?"

Holding his record under his jacket, he went to the counter and put down the other two. He saw the woman watching him, amused, and he said, "I think the machine's busted. I didn't do it, but it—" He stopped when he heard the limp, loose-jointed music coming from the booth. He didn't know what to say.

The woman took the two records from him. "You probably didn't know how to work it. I'm afraid the girls will be in there quite awhile."

He looked at the woman's pinched face. His nerves were knotting the muscles in his thighs, and when he saw the girls ganging around the booth again, he knew he'd have to find out about the record soon, or not at all. The sweat was running down his neck, over the short, jutting collarbones, and the inside of his nose was sore. He had to take a chance. "Look, can you show me how to play this?" He took his record from its torn wrapping and handed it to her.

She examined it closely on both sides. "Was this what you were trying to play? No wonder. This is seventy-eight r.p.m. The machine is for long-playing." She gave it back to him.

He didn't know what she meant. "This is no good?"

She laughed. "You have to use a turntable that goes faster, like this one." She pointed to a small machine at the end of the counter.

Reminding himself that he had to hear this, had to know, he took another chance. "Can I try it just for a minute? It's important." She wouldn't know anything about the people involved, any more than he would. If the record started saying things that were too important, he could shut it off and get out. But he had to hear once.

She hesitated. "Well, I guess it will be all right." She walked over to the small player. "I'm certainly doing a large business this afternoon." The music from the booth rose up and rattled, then sank back again.

Charlie gave her the record, and she turned on a switch and waited for the thing to warm up. She said, "This isn't a commercial record. No label, too small."

He didn't say anything. He watched her put the record on and adjust the needle at the edge, and he closed his eyes, intending to concentrate on every sound. He tried to shut away the music.

A stern old man's voice, speaking from far back in the throat, said, "Delson, this paper has independent views, and you know it."

A younger voice, thin and nasal, said, "Sure, I know, sir. Everybody's got to take a stand this time of year, this year."

"Granted. We'll take ours soon."

The young voice said, "We want you. And we're prepared to thank you, in a big way."

A pause. The old man said, "That's interesting."

The younger man cleared his throat. It made the record scratch. "Here's the story. We're going to lick the Senator, even though he looks pretty well licked already. Now you've always been a fine, healthy, sane influence on this part of the country, and if you help us we'll reward you."

The old man's voice was quiet, careful. "What did you have in mind?"

"A controlling interest in that New York paper you've always had your eye on."

"And I'm supposed to ... ?"

"You know. Gut the Senator, plug us. We can give you plenty of the right sort of material. That's all we ask."

The old man's voice was louder. "Well, it wouldn't be hard to flush that bastard."

The woman behind the counter said, "Well, my goodness."

Charlie waved his hand at her. He kept listening.

The younger voice said, "We can't put the agreement in writing, sir, but if we get in, you can count on us. My chief told me to assure you."

"His word's okay with me. But tell him if I'm going to blast the Senator, that'll mean I have to listen to the son-of-a-bitch blather at me over the radio, and I'll need something to offset that." He chuckled.

The woman behind the counter said, "Take that record away this instant. I never heard such language." She reached for it, but Charlie grabbed her arm.

He said, "Just another minute, please."

The young man's voice said, "I have an outline of some of the things that we ... "

The woman nearly shouted, "Take your hands off me."

Charlie kept trying to listen, kept trying to keep other things away, but he saw that all the girls had come out of the booth and were staring at him. The fat girl came toward the counter with her mouth open.

Charlie said, "It's all right. Never mind."

The fat girl leaned over the machine on the counter. "Party records?" Her eyes were wide.

The old man's voice said, "How much of this is true?"

Raising her head and biting her lower lip, the woman behind the counter swung at Charlie with her free hand. "Get out or I'll call the police."

The girls began to chatter.

Charlie gave up. He took the record off the machine, hearing the needle rake over the little grooves, and he tried to slide it back into the crumpled envelope.

The fat girl said, "Do you sell those things, mister?"

The woman rubbed her wrist and looked at it. "Try to do someone a favor." The end of her nose was white, and one curl of her dark hair had come unswept. It dangled over her ear. "Get out of here immediately. You should be thankful I don't call my father from next door. He'd show you how to treat a lady."

Charlie started for the door, keeping his eyes away from them all. His legs were shaking again, and he couldn't stay in a straight line.

The fat girl said, "I've got a record-player at home, mister. Nobody's there now."

Another girl said, "Some music-lover."

His hand was slippery on the doorknob, but after two twists, he got it open and was out on the brilliant pavement. Because he didn't dare stop for a minute, in case the woman did call her father or the police, he walked west along the same side of the street, going as fast as he could, and keeping his legs stiff. Couldn't do one thing right. He remembered almost all the men had said on the record, but he couldn't put it together with what had happened to him. The old man worked on a newspaper or owned it. Maybe it was the same paper Lily worked on, if she'd really been a reporter. But he still didn't know which one it was. Some funny dealings going on. One name: Delson. He'd have to remember that. Bribery and a Senator they didn't like. Nothing about any R.Q. or a briefcase. Nothing about a stout, middle-aged woman with glasses who had been jockeyed out of a train. Nothing about two men in the dark. Nothing about murder.

He saw a bar in the next block, and dragging his safety shoes up over the curb of a cross-street, he made for it. A glass of beer now, off the street, out of sight. Somewhere dingy and cool. His throat felt cracked inside, and his hands dead and wet under the bulk of his jacket. Some place quiet where people wouldn't talk to him, and where he could make everything yesterday for a little while.

He came to the door of the bar and looked back over his shoulder at the stretch of sidewalk toward the record shop. No one was following. He'd have to be more careful, because if he ever got tangled with the police, they'd look at his wallet, find his name, and that would finish it. He pushed the heavy glass door open and walked in. The room was dim, cold, and nearly empty, and as he looked around, making sure there were no policemen catching a quick one, he smelled the familiar mixture of leather and beer. It soothed him immediately, cooled the inside of his chest, and he went to the end of the bar and sat on a leather-topped stool. He laid a dollar out flat on the shiny wood and held up one finger. The bartender brought a glass of beer.

He still didn't know anything, and he felt weak and useless in the face of all the things that were happening. He needed help. As he sat, sipping the beer and washing his tongue with it, he tried to think of someone who might help him. He hadn't lived in South Chicago for three years. No telling who was left of the easy friends he'd once known. No relatives, besides the too-talkative Aunt Myra. Well, there was old Uncle Art who ran a drugstore in Joliet, but Art scarcely knew what time it was any more. His mother dead, and she wouldn't have known how to help anyway. A couple of switchmen who used to work near the steel mills. Joe Blake and Duffer. Might try them, but they were as dumb as he was. He concentrated. Couldn't think of anyone, else. He'd never made many friends; too quiet, too calm. There were some out in the Indiana suburbs around Whiting and Hammond, but he didn't dare go in that direction. They wanted him there. He finished the beer and waved for another one.

The bartender was a sleek-looking man with broad shoulders and hair that made him look taller than he was. He slid the beer toward Charlie, slopping the foam out onto the bar and Charlie's hand.

The bartender pulled his wide lips down and winked. "Sorry."

Charlie smiled, then sneezed. It was too cold with the air-conditioning. "That's all right." He wiped his nose on his sleeve. "It's awful cold in here."

"You're telling me? I got sinus trouble from it."

Charlie felt the sweat on the back of his shirt burning like ice against his shoulder blades. He'd probably catch cold, but it didn't matter. It would be warm in jail, and he'd get to eat a lot of soup. Having run out of ideas, he accepted the fact that he'd be arrested any minute. Nothing he could do.

The bartender began to wipe the other end of the bar with a long white cloth, and Charlie took the pictures of checks out of his jacket pocket and looked at them. Why would anybody want to kill a woman just to get these? He read the names on each of the three pictures, but none of them was Delson and none of them anything like R. Q. He'd never seen such big sums of money written down at once on a check: one was $2500, another $5630, the last $8750. He looked more closely at the largest: it was made out to Chalmers Bergnauer and was signed illegibly by somebody. He'd never heard of the man before. He could be one of the two men who'd chased him, but how could he ever find out? Pictures of checks didn't prove anything, and the police would probably laugh at him if he tried to tell how he found them.

He glanced up and saw his own face in the mirror, then looked away quickly. He didn't like to look at his face, especially not in bars. But the image of the close-together cheekbones, the dark, stringy hair, and the thin mouth that drooped, stayed with him even when he stared at the door to the ladies' john. He wished he were somebody else. Somebody bigger, different, who had fists like jugs and legs like fireplugs, who wasn't afraid of trains and things. Wishing didn't do any good. He was still too little, and he was getting afraid again.

When he saw the telephone on the far wall, he didn't know at first that he'd already started to think. But when he looked down at the checks and then at the phone again, the idea was there, complete. He got off the stool, feeling his legs flutter as he put his weight on them, and he walked slowly back to the ledge where the phonebooks were. Using the small yellow light there, he thumbed through the Chicago directory, heisting his jacket up under his arm and holding the checks so that he could see. He found the name: Chalmers Bergnauer. And for several moments he stared at the number. He wasn't good at this kind of thing, but he had to do something. It couldn't hurt. No one could call the police this way.

The phone was not in a booth, and he hesitated for a moment. He didn't like being out in the open. Playing the record in front of other people had been a mistake, and the bartender was sure to hear what he said. Taking a deep breath of the chilled air that rushed around him, he decided to do it anyway. Bartenders minded their own business usually. He dialed the number and waited, not sure what he was going to say.

A woman with a slow, tired voice answered. "The Bergnauers' residence."

Charlie spoke through his teeth. "Speak to Mr. Bergnauer, please?"

"Who's calling?"

He could tell she didn't really care. "A friend." The bartender was rattling a new sack of ice cubes into a little bin.

The woman said, "He's not at home right now. You can reach him at his office."

Charlie wiped his forehead with his free hand and pressed the receiver closer to his ear. "Can you give me the number? I'm from some place else—I mean, out of town."

She said, "Yes." Her voice was further away, and she droned the number.

He hung up without thanking her, because he had to keep saying the number to himself to remember it. After the coin dropped, he put in another, still mumbling to himself, and he nearly forgot the exchange word as he peered closely at the numbers and letters inside the holes of the dial.

This time a man answered, his voice sour and fast. "Yes, what is it?"

Charlie held his teeth together, hoping. "Mr. Bergnauer?"

"Yes. Who's speaking?"

Charlie concentrated. "Lily's dead."

The man's words grew more clipped. "Lily who?"

"You know: Lily. She's got the briefcase."

"Say, what's all this about?"

Charlie fished around wildly. "Well, never mind. I just wanted you to know I've got a check you cashed for eighty-seven hundred and fifty dollars. You remember?"

The man didn't answer.

Charlie could hear the wires buzzing, far away, and for a moment, he thought the man at the other end had hung up. But then he spoke again, his voice softer, too nice.

He said, "Is this some kind of hold-up?"

Charlie didn't know. He said, "I don't know."

There was a pause. The man said, "Look, I wonder if you could hold the line just a minute. There's somebody here I have to get rid of. Okay? You just hold on, and I'll be right with you."

Charlie wanted to call him back, tell him that it didn't matter, that nothing made any difference. It wasn't going to work. But he waited anyway, and he heard someone shuffling around at the other end. The receiver clicked several times in his ear. In a sudden panic, he hung up, picked up his jacket, put the checks back into the pocket, and headed for the door. Maybe the man was trying to trace the call or something. And the police would be careening down 71st Street to the door of the bar. He looked, from the corner of his eye, at the bartender, but he was wiping glasses, not paying any attention. At the door, he tried to see through the thick panes, but it was all brightness, no people. And then, limping, he stepped outside, and the heat of the day slammed in around him again, and all the cold air from the bar ran from his mouth and nose.

He stood on the sidewalk, waiting for his breath to come back. He looked at the clock in the window of a shop next door: 3:10. The eastbound express would be due any minute to flash by his crossing and rock the ground under him, to murder the weed-groves with its dust, to send his hair flying, legs shaking. No. That was some place else. He called himself back and looked at the empty IC tracks. That was yesterday. Now, people were running after him, and the next edition of the evening paper would be on the newsstands soon. He looked back the way he'd come and saw a stand he had passed without noticing. Have to get a paper to know what to do. Maybe by this time the police had caught the two men and put them away. Or maybe they'd found out who Lily was. He started to walk in that direction, while the sun baked his shoulders and curled the hairs on the back of his neck.

When he got to the stand, he saw that the later edition was out already, and he bought one without looking at the man or at anyone who passed. Had to do it that way, or else he'd try to run. He didn't look at the newspaper either. Instead, he walked slowly toward a movie theater in the middle of the block. Dark there, and maybe not so cold or hot. He bought a ticket with the change in his pocket, and didn't raise his eyes to meet those of the girl in the glass booth. Something wrong with booths. Only when he was inside, in the near darkness of the cross aisle at the rear, did he look at the paper, and as the screen suddenly turned very bright with a shot of snow and tobogganers, he saw his picture, larger than his fist, on the upper half of the front page.

CHAPTER FOUR

The fatty ruins of two orders of pork shanks lay strewn in and out of shallow bowls, and four steins, two empty and two half full of dark beer, cluttered the spaces between boiled potatoes and dishes of red cabbage. Using his spoon between the small dish and the bread, Milan Praksar spread a thin piece of pumpernickel with what once had been butter.

Cooper said, "He'll be here in a couple minutes. You just keep your face shut."

"Yeah, yeah." Cooper always made such a big deal out of everything. Big showdown every time you turned around.

Cooper said, "He's seen the paper. I could tell by his voice on the phone. He'll be ready to play ball."

Praksar didn't care. The boiled potatoes were getting cold, but salt, pepper, and the specks of parsley made them interesting enough to chew for a long time. Then if you took a mouthful of dark beer, the mixture was crazy. "Who cares?"

"You like money?"

Because Cooper looked insulted, Praksar said, "Sure."

"Everything's going to be okay."

For the seventh or eighth time, Praksar glanced at the woman seated two tables away. He couldn't make up his mind. Sometimes she looked good enough to try for, sometimes not. Her straight, dark hair was parted in the middle and her face would pass, but maybe she was too skinny. Maybe her breasts were just barely too small to trouble about.

Cooper said, "Here he comes. Look, he's nervous as a fruit."

Praksar looked. The sunlight, through tall shutters, rammed a series of gold bars between them and the restaurant entrance, and he could see Hindruth walking fast through them. He had a newspaper under one arm.

Cooper said, "Remember, you keep out of it."

Hindruth came up to the table, hesitated, started to sit down, didn't, started to say something, didn't, then sat down. He put the newspaper on the dirty tablecloth.

Cooper said, "Hi."

Leaning forward out of the shafts of light, Hindruth looked straight at Cooper. "I'd like a word with you."

Cooper put a dab of butter on a piece of boiled potato. "I'm eating right now, mister."

"Don't give me that."

Praksar looked at them both, amused. Cooper would probably rib the guy plenty now, and the little, gray-haired jerk wouldn't be able to take it. All kinds of funny things might happen. He hadn't been in a fight for a long time.

Cooper said, "Well, all right. I guess this can wait a bit." He wiped more grease on his mouth with his napkin.

After glancing nervously at the nearby tables and at the single waiter, bald and small, standing near a stack of dirty dishes on the other side of the room, Hindruth said, "Have you seen the newspapers?"

Cooper nodded. "That crossing guy has himself in dutch with everybody."

Hindruth reached over and touched Cooper's dark coat-sleeve with his fist. "Who killed that woman, you or Praksar?"

"You shouldn't go saying things like that. Not right out." Cooper's voice was hurt. "I told you what happened. That's all.

That crossing guy, Bell, he's the one who done it. Why should I want to knock her off?"

"Why should he?"

Praksar grunted. He couldn't enjoy his eating. Making all this fuss over a dame and a mousy guy who'd jump forty feet if you said yah to him.

Gesturing with a fork, Cooper said, "How'd I know? Maybe he raped her. Anyways, you can be damned glad the cops are cracking after him. He'll have a tough time unloading the record and those checks on any newspaper, and don't tell me that ain't a good thing. All we got to hope is they catch him. We can buy cops in that hick suburb a quarter apiece, and nobody wiser."

Hindruth was quiet for a moment. "You know what a murder charge would do to this outfit?"

Cooper said, "Sure I know. You think I'm nuts? Last time I seen that woman she was out cold, but she was alive. And Bell was with her. You figure it out. The cops want him, not me. And Praksar was in South Chicago, screwing around looking for a car."

Praksar said, "Yeah. It was Bell all right." And Cooper kicked him under the table. Kicked him right in the shin with the side of his shoe. "God damn it."

"Shut up."

Hindruth said, "This better be the truth."

Lifting one shoulder, Cooper said, "Believe what you want to. Tell you what: I got an idea, and we'll see about it later. Now, my food's getting cold." With knife and fork he began searching through pork fat for slivers of meat.

"I'm busy. If you've got an idea, say it now." Hindruth picked up his newspaper and pushed his chair back a little.

On the other hand, sometimes the ones without a front porch were the wildest of all. Praksar stared hard at the woman, trying to make her look his way. Maybe if he caught her straight in the eye, he could tell. He put a forkful of red cabbage into his mouth and found Cooper and Hindruth both looking at him. Had he missed something? He searched his mind wildly for something to say. "This *kapusta* tastes like crud."

Hindruth said, "What's he for? What does he do?"

Cooper smiled. "Anything."

Feeling embarrassed and a little angry, Praksar said, "I'm sorta the brains for Cooper." But it only made him feel worse: some of the cabbage came out of the side of his mouth and hung there.

Hindruth said, "What did you two do out East? As though I didn't know."

With a wave of his hand Cooper said, "Oh, we did a little work for the Senator. And some other guys."

"Ever been to Chicago before?"

Getting the cabbage back where it belonged, Praksar decided he'd been quiet long enough. Couldn't let a nowhere like Hindruth get him edgy. "Sure. Once me and Cooper helped Mossy ... " The same spot on his shin jolted again. "Aw, knock it off, Cooper. You tryin' to crack my leg? I wasn't gonna say nothin'. I was gonna lie."

Cooper smiled with half his face. "Don't mind him, Hindruth. It's nice to have somebody around who never worries. He doesn't have anything to worry with."

"You don't have to convince me. Now I can give you two more minutes. What's the large idea?"

Cooper leaned over the table. "Look, here's what I figured on doing: we ought to keep our eyes on the newspaper offices in town. The bad ones, I mean. That way we might catch this Bell guy if he tries to peddle his papers, and we can talk him out of it. Or beat him out of it."

"You think he'll go for the newspapers?"

"I'd bet anything. What else is he going to do? If mugs like him don't go to the cops right away, they don't go at all. Believe me, I know. Either he'll try a newspaper, or he'll head way the hell away from here."

Hindruth frowned. "If he committed a murder, why should he run to tell some reporter?"

Praksar laughed, choked, and drank some beer. Cooper wasn't so smart either. A real busher.

Hurriedly Cooper said, "He might try it for two reasons: first, maybe he killed the dame by accident. Only a newspaper would believe him right away with a story like that. Makes a *good* story, see? Circulation. Cops would laugh like hell at him. Or he thinks so. Second, if he done it on purpose—killed her, I mean—maybe he figures the record and checks are a good out, good enough to let him shift everything on us. Of course, he may just take off like a big-ass bird. But we can't be sure."

Hindruth fanned himself with his newspaper, looked at it, then looked up. "All right. Go ahead. We can't take a chance. Anyway, don't just sit here."

Steadily, not moving, not trying to sell it, Cooper said, "We'll have to hire somebody else to help. Maybe a private cop. Two guys can't watch three places, you know."

Praksar smiled. Same old Cooper. Swindle his old lady on the price of milk.

"All right, all right."

Cooper said, "I'll need a little dough."

Praksar caught Cooper's blankest, hardest look while Hindruth fished in his wallet, but he kept smiling. It was funny how some guys couldn't even spit without being cagey about it.

Hindruth handed over another hundred. "There aren't many of these, you know. The Senator's a millionaire, but he doesn't let it show very often."

"Sure."

Hindruth stood up. "I've got to go. And you'd better go too. It's a cinch Bell won't be coming in here."

Cooper emptied his glass of beer. "Sure thing." And as Hindruth walked away, he called after him. "And keep that mail in the black, boy."

They nudged each other below the tablecloth, carefully not laughing, as Hindruth froze, almost turned around, then went on toward the swinging door.

Praksar said, "Jesus, is he scared!"

While putting the money away, Cooper pulled out some coins to leave a tip. "That's the way we should keep him. Let's get out of here."

Praksar looked at the woman who showed no signs of leaving and who still wouldn't turn his way. "What's the rush? It ain't even dark yet." But he got up when Cooper did and started meandering with him toward the cashier. Hell, even the little bit she had under the flashy silk print was probably phony. For the birds.

Belching gently, Cooper said, "She was on the *Evening News*, right?"

"Right."

"What'd you do with her pocketbook?"

Praksar laughed to himself, remembering how funny Cooper had looked, hauling the dame out of the shed full of ice and fish behind the restaurant, nearly rupturing himself getting her into the alley and into the car. Like a lady wrestler.

"Thrun it in with the lobsters, like you said. Do they eat things?"

"Forget it." Cooper paid the bill, and they went through the door into the massive heat.

The lines of cut-rate, out-of-business shambles and the grimy people standing in doorways made the neighborhood feel like home. Praksar picked his teeth.

Cooper said, "The next edition's out." He pointed to a news-shanty where the papers were clipped to a wire that ran along the front. He walked over and bought one.

Praksar read the middle part of a left-hand-column, front-page story over Cooper's shoulder: "…named Charles Bell. She was identified almost by accident by a Hammond reporter at the Lake County Morgue. Chicagoans will remember Lily Gonchar's controversial articles in the *Evening News* on local political corruption last year. Police are trying to trace her movements of yesterday, but have reported nothing so far. Bell, the crossing watchman, is still missing. Chief Rakovitch has given no indication of a motive for the crime."

The paper was making hot stuff out of the murder of its lady reporter. Praksar didn't read any more. They were just fishing around. He leaned closer and looked at the picture beside the story, and he studied the narrow cheeks, the wet, dark eyes, the rumpled hair, and the chin that came to a point like the unbitten end of a big cigar. It was the face of a kid who'd just been kicked, one of those second-hand kids that just hang around places. He didn't have to look twice. He'd remember. He knew that kind. They might throw something or holler once, maybe only stick out their tongues, but they'd run. Always run. You didn't have to worry. They never did anything. You could find one near every garbage can in Jersey. No guts. None of them could thumb their noses and stay put. They ran. Or if they got brave and stayed, their fists were like doughnuts. They never learned not to give a damn.

Cooper said, "Let's go."

Pleased at finding himself thinking about something, Praksar followed. "Do I get some of that dough?"

"Keep your pants on."

And they'd always get blamed for everything. Anything.

CHAPTER FIVE

Closing the door of the men's room behind him, Charlie groped past a dim red Coke machine at the back of the theater and went toward a door marked as an exit. He felt in his pocket for his watch, then remembered it was lying in his apartment, broken, beyond use, and when he looked around him, past the water fountain, above the balcony stairs, he couldn't see a clock. Well, he couldn't stay in the movie any longer. He'd seen the feature once and a half, had stayed in the john for as long as he could stand the stronger light. It ought to be dark outside by this time, maybe dark enough for him to go unrecognized.

At the exit, he realized he still had the newspaper in his hand, and he stuffed it endwise into a tall cigarette urn, wishing every edition of it for miles around the same finish. He almost knew the story by heart, and the fact that Lily was a real person, even well-known, made him feel both more important and more afraid.

Letting the door close, he walked down the sloping outer lobby to the street entrance, and halfway there, he saw that it was still light outside, no longer with yellow sunlight but with a kind of flushed gray. He stopped and wanted to go back into the dark, but when he saw the usher leaning on a waist-high ticket box, watching him, he knew he couldn't; and he turned away from the people who were just coming in, kept his face to one side, and went out to the sidewalk and around the corner.

The air was not as warm as it had been, but he wouldn't dare put on his jacket and turn up the collar. Bake himself, and attract attention. He found the nearest doorway of a closed shop and stepped into it, wanting to lie down and sleep. Daylight Saving Time. He could never get used to it, no matter how many months went by. His instinct was geared to something near sun time, but the way clocks flipped backwards and forwards had ruined it, and he began to feel really uneasy for the first time at the hopelessness of being without a watch. Now, looking around the corner of the plate glass at the western sky, he guessed it at after 7:30, clock time.

Only one thing to do. He left the doorway and walked as fast as he could down the inside of the sidewalk toward the first cross street. The long rest in the movie had eased his legs, and they scarcely hurt at all, even when he stretched them to full stride. Coming to the corner, he put his free hand over his mouth and nose, edged around two men who were arguing with each other, and turned north in the direction of Jackson Park.

Lily had worked for the *Evening News*. She'd had something to do with politics, and that was what the record and the pictures of checks were about. She'd been killed because of them. So the only thing he could do that might help save him was to find a friend of Lily at the newspaper. The friend might know what the briefcase stuff meant, might believe a story that a crossing watchman couldn't dream up by himself, might be honest, might know somebody.

The evening traffic was heavy on the through street beside him, but no one else was on the sidewalk. For a moment, he thought wistfully of the IC trains back on 71st Street. Much quicker to get downtown that way. But people on the trains read newspapers, had them there in their hands to compare faces with, and the conductors had learned to be nosey to keep awake. Better to hitch-hike onto the Outer Drive. An out-of-town car, someone on a trip who didn't have time to think about murder.

After the long blocks, the curve to the right, and the stop-light, his legs began to hurt again, and he stopped at curbside, watching the many lanes meet and most of the cars go humping over the short, blunt bridge beside the tree-shaded lagoon where the sailboats and yachts were moored. He walked further till he was opposite the bridge, then crossed the road, half at a try, hoping all the drivers were blind, wishing he still had his red handkerchief so he could blow his nose all the time.

At the other side, he went up the arching sidewalk of the bridge and down to a level again. He knew there had been a policeman directing traffic behind him at the intersection, but he'd refused to admit it. Had to do it this way. Couldn't let the fear really start, go jumping, truss up his legs and knot the thigh muscles, cripple his hands. Had to walk, think of the Loop, of West Madison. The office of the *Evening News* was there. He remembered seeing it once.

He walked to the first slight curve in the road where a smaller lane led back into the park. Waiting there in the long shadows from the trees on the other side, he watched the cars go by. At first, they were so close together that the fast whish as each passed sounded like the breaks between cars of a passenger train, and he felt that he had to hold up his jacket like a warning sign. But when the spaces widened and the soft grass under his feet gave as he shifted his weight, he remembered what he had to do. He stared up the road, waited for strange colors on license plates, and stuck out his thumb.

The next stream of cars contained a motorcycle cop, and Charlie pulled in his arm, turned away. The motorcycle sped past, and he watched it weave in and out of traffic around the curve and out of sight. They were going to be everywhere. Might as well get used to it, forget to be too careful.

When he saw the old dusty blue Plymouth come over the little bridge at the tail end of the line of cars and noticed the odd blue-and-orange license, he hitched his thumb again and managed to smile. It was going more slowly than the others, and as it passed him, he saw the old woman who was driving look his way. The car pulled to the curb ahead of him and stopped. He went to the open door, knowing that it was taking him too long to walk.

The old woman said, "Get in, hurry. I'll get run over."

He slid onto the worn seat-covers, folded his jacket in his lap, and slammed the door shut. The sun visor from over the inside of the windshield fell down between his knees.

The old woman said, "Don't pay no attention." She started the car in second, and it bucked out to the middle of the road, jamming the traffic behind it.

Charlie tried to get the sun visor back onto its metal rod. "I'm sorry." The felt socket of the visor was tattered and wouldn't fit.

The old woman laughed, a firm, deep grunting, surprisingly loud. "Just keep your elbow on the side window. It's kind of tricky too."

Putting his arm up as a brace, he looked at the woman. She had a large jaw that went down into a tangle of stringy lace at her throat, and her gray hair was thrust here and there, mostly under a small red hat which was woven of something as stiff as horsehair. The front seat was pushed up close to the dashboard, and her thick legs straddled the steering column, hauling her long dark dress back to her knees. He didn't feel very comfortable.

She said, "Where you going? I always like to give servicemen a lift." She glanced at him around her dimesized glasses.

"Downtown." Old ladies always made him want to be very polite, but he didn't know how to act with this one. "I'm not in the Army."

She said, "You don't have to be in the *Army*." She began to hum something.

The car went under an overhead cross-walk and came out onto the wide drive along Lake Michigan where the beaches, below the level of the road, bent around north to the high breakwater rocks. He could see, down the drive and to the left, the tall apartment houses begin to flash with light.

She said, "Are you going home?"

He looked at her, surer than ever that she couldn't possibly know who he was, and he said, "No." No, wherever that was.

"Well, have a good time." She drove in the outside lane, and the other cars passed continuously at twice her speed. "I'm going to see my sister in Chicago. Never been here before." She smiled, and her jaw came up out of the lace.

Looking over his shoulder, Charlie saw that the back seat was filled with boxes and loose clothing. The window rattled against his elbow. "I hope you have a real nice time too."

"Thanks. I always say folks don't never get too old." The front wheel nicked the curb, and the car lunged out into the next lane, forcing two cabs to veer and nearly touch fenders.

Though he felt certain that she was a little crazy, he found himself liking this woman. She didn't worry about things, not even driving. "That's right. You got to act like you can't stop moving. Then pretty soon you can't." He didn't know what he was talking about, but it felt good to tell her something that sounded wise. All he needed was a glass of beer, and he could think of other things.

She said, "It's like this here car. My son said it wouldn't go nowhere. Well, it did, and I've druv it all the way from Tyrone, Pennsylvania."

They went over a small rise in the highway, and Charlie looked out over the water at a sailboat, leaning with the wind and turning slowly toward an artificial cove. He said, "It's pretty here."

"Is it? What does it look like?"

He watched her swivel the steering wheel back and forth and squint through the bug-spattered windshield, and he remembered she probably couldn't see very well. "Oh, there's all that water and the rocks." He didn't know what it was that made things pretty. Taking a deep breath, he smelled the clean lake as the air rushed in at him through the vent. No oil or scum here. No railroad tracks. Just the smell of water, and no fish.

She said, "I used to get all flighty 'cause I couldn't see things good. But after my husband died, there wasn't nothing worth looking at. He was funny."

Charlie sat still for a long time, letting his arm get cramped, and the blurred hulk of Soldier Field rose up ahead of them. She had good strong legs. He saw how they lolled sideways, then arched occasionally to tramp on the brake for no apparent reason. She wore raggedy slippers that bulged at the instep, but she could probably run if she had to, and she could jump up and down. He felt his own legs, waiting for them to throb, but they didn't.

He said, "I wonder can you let me off in the Loop somewheres?"

She pushed her shoulders back against the seat till it popped, and stiffened her arms while she yawned. "Well, I think so. My sister lives at the Friday House. It's a hotel. I just drive straight into town and turn a couple times. She told me how."

"You mean the Farraday House?"

"Well, something like that." She smiled and looked over at him.

Several cars honked behind them, and she took the next broad curve at the Aquarium gradually, going from lane to lane.

Charlie didn't look or say anything. He felt safe as long as the windows were dirty, and the hard, clear smell of the woman reassured him, made him want to keep rocking as the car took the swells in the road.

She said, "Are you married?"

Because the worries had quit circling around the inside of his ears like worms, it was easy to answer. "No."

She clucked. "Is your wife in the service?"

He felt the whole evening grow a little more vague. "No. I don't think so." He paused. "I said I wasn't married."

"Oh, *I see*. Well, that's all right."

He closed his eyes as they started down the very broad run to the east of Grant Park and the Chicago skyline. It didn't matter whether the old woman knew where she was going or not. He'd let her drop him where she felt like, and he'd stay there for a while and keep forgetting the last two days. The air was cool as water, and the car rattled gently, not swerving now or snorting. He dozed off.

She said, "Well, we've come into something."

He woke up and saw Michigan Avenue, jumbled and crisscrossed by buses, cabs, and people, and the policeman standing beside the safety island was looking at their car. He slumped in his seat.

She said, "We come to a kind of bridge, and I knew that wasn't right. My sister didn't say nothing about that. I turned in a ways, and here we are." She smiled and waved out the window at the policeman. "I like to be nice, but most folks don't get to be very nice back."

Charlie put his hand over the lower part of his face and stared to one side at the flat, colorless reflection of his own shoulder in the window glass. "Just go straight in."

"All right. It won't take me a minute to find places." She jerked the gearshift back and went through the stuffed-together traffic between the tall buildings.

After she had turned several corners, stopped, started, blown the horn briefly, and laughed once, Charlie looked up again. No more policemen in sight. The fear had come again in a moment, had come as hard as ever before, and he felt silly with weakness. He must have been crazy to come here into the crowds and the police, some even on horses. But it still didn't matter too much. The worst he could do was get caught. "You can let me out wherever you stop next."

She pushed her glasses up the bridge of her nose with her forefinger. "Well, I'm just liable to stop most anywhere, so you better point." Pulling close to the curb till the car tipped side-ways in the deep gutter, she let the motor idle behind a couple of pausing taxis.

Charlie opened the door, and it scraped its bottom on the foot-high cement. He began to edge himself backwards through the narrow slit, trying to put his legs on something level so they wouldn't twist. "This'll be fine. I can get there from here."

Putting her large, red hand on the car seat, she leaned on it and looked up at him. "Don't go getting into fights now, you hear? I read pretty near everybody fights with each other in this town. Well, not you."

"No." He looked at the way the flesh dimpled on the top of her wrist and at each knuckle. "I never fight anybody."

She said, "Good-by. It's been real nice, wherever you are." She leaned a little further, and the car bucked and stalled as her foot came off the clutch.

The door slammed itself shut, and though he was unwilling to leave her in what might be a jam, he walked away; and when she started the car again and banged into the rear of a cab and the policeman on the far corner looked up and took a few steps their way, Charlie walked even faster among the people, through the tangled lights of the restaurant and shop-fronts. He kept his head down and followed the crowd to the corner, waited with them for the light, crossed State Street, turned and crossed to the south side of Madison, and went down it to the middle of the block.

There, where fewer people walked the sidewalk and where all the advertising signs from behind, ahead, and both sides shed their light, he went more slowly, knowing he'd have to do something about his face. It had been in the papers. He'd seen it there, the picture he'd had taken for the yard-office files when the insurance claim for his legs had been wandering through the dusty, moneyless hands in the central division, beyond postcards, beyond phone-calls. It looked too much like him, embarrassed him every time he saw it. His mother, had she been able to poke her head up out of the ground to see it, would have called it sweet. That was the trouble. He knew his face looked like that, but it didn't seem right to have everybody know he was forty-six years old and sometimes looked eighteen.

But now it was more than that. He had to change himself or he might not even get as far as the *Evening News* office. Had to gimmick himself up with a mask or something; the paper hadn't said anything about his clothes.

He walked further down the street, keeping out of the way as much as possible. Most of the stores were closed, but he came to one that was still lighted. Above the open door was a badly painted sign: Factory Surplus Outlet; and little electric bulbs were strung all along the outside, yellowing the jumble of odds and ends boxed carelessly inside the window. He saw all kinds of hats and baseball caps there, costume jewelry, socks. A hat would help: shadow his face, keep it from looking as long and narrow as in the picture.

Waiting at the corner of the store, outside the full range of the lights, he looked at the man sitting on a stool between the heaped tables. The man might recognize him, bring everything to a finish with one shout, yet he was taking that much of a chance every time he passed somebody on the street. But after he got a hat, he'd be safer. Making sure that no one else was in the store at the moment, he went through the door, and with his back to the street he rummaged among some straw hats.

The man slid off his stool and came over to Charlie's side. "Something in the line of hats? Got some out-size bargains. Stuff maybe a little paper around the crown, and you got yourself a ten-dollar panama: one ninety-eight."

Charlie just looked at the hats. He waited for the man to act suspicious, to try something. He could get away pretty fast. But the man didn't do anything, and Charlie said, "I more likely need a baseball cap."

The man was dark and pudgy, his face screwed back into a fixed knuckling-under expression. His bald head, interlaced with thin, wet hair, came only to Charlie's shoulder. He said, "We got plenty baseball caps, all kinds. Take a look." He led the way over to another table.

Though he kept his eye on the door, Charlie didn't see anyone even pausing as though he might come in. He followed the man to a matted, twisted stack of caps and glanced hurriedly at the various light and dark colors. He picked up a duck-billed blue one and tried it on.

The man said, "Forty-eight cents. Bargain, believe me."

"All right." He got a dollar out of his pocket and looked around, feeling that the cap wouldn't be good enough by itself. Needed something else.

The man held his palm out tentatively for the dollar, but when Charlie didn't give it to him right away, he said, "Got some fine socks. Factory makes a little mistake in them, but who notices? Eighteen cents a pair."

Charlie saw a box crammed full of sunglasses, and he knew they'd be what he needed. Blot out his eyes. "A pair of them." He pointed.

Taking up a handful, the man tried a few on himself. "See? Like expensive ones. Keep from burning your eyes out at the ball game. Twenty-three cents, any pair."

After trying two whose temples bit at his ears, Charlie found a pair that stayed without hurting. Everything was darker, but not dark enough to be sleepy or dangerous. "I'll take the both." He handed over the dollar.

Fumbling in the change box, the man said, "You baseball fan?"

Charlie took his quarter and four pennies and didn't say anything. He went toward the door, and the man told him to come again in a sad voice.

It had worked, and nothing was wrong yet. With the duck bill pulled down till the inside of it touched the tops of his glasses, he walked past the refuse can and the squat mailbox at the next corner, and he didn't glance from side to side to see whether someone was coming to grab his arm. Because all the lights he saw were cut to one-third of their brightness, he had the feeling that other people wouldn't be able to see well either. Or if they did look closely, maybe they'd think he'd hurt his eyes, ruined them getting a suntan or something.

As he went further west, the scurry of people thinned, the stores became larger companies, wholesalers, and the lights were all either high overhead or from cars at his side. Two more blocks and he came to the brief uphill slant that led to the bridge over the Chicago River. Every time a car passed now, it rattled the boards and metal slats of the bridge, and he walked beside the short, arching metal girders and crossed the middle where the two halves didn't fit well. He shuffled his feet carefully at the break, then stepped over it, feeling like a blindman. The smell of the river was not the smell of the lake: here the water clogged the back of his mouth with fumes from everything dead in the city. Though he couldn't see the surface even when he leaned over the side of the bridge, he knew it scarcely moved, held its blackness and its grease permanently. He breathed out hard through his nose and started down the slope of the other side.

On the real sidewalk again, he stopped and pushed his glasses down. Ahead, on the opposite side of the street, he saw the big *Evening News* building and the railroad station beyond. This was almost the place, and there had to be something to do. Settling his glasses, he walked slowly down the long block till he came to the dark, in-jutting doorway of a plumber's shop; he stepped sideways into it and waited for a moment, watching.

The building was well lighted and busy: out of the broad main doors came men in light straw hats and sport shirts, and others passed them on the way in. As long as he had his sunglasses on, they all looked alike. Paper trucks pulled in and out of the side street beyond, and their motors coughed between the building and the station. He didn't know what to do. Those men, though he couldn't see their faces, acted like foreigners to everything he knew about; yet if he could believe their newspaper, they were very interested in him, wanted him, maybe hated his guts, would give a lot for a chance to talk to him. And all because of Lily, a woman who'd been hit over the head, and he especially didn't understand her. What had he planned to do? Well, talk to one or two of them, perhaps just hint at things. The jacket over his arm still had the slips of paper in it and the record. But how could he ever say things right, like they happened? He wasn't even sure what had happened. And they'd have the police there before he could find words to hack it out with.

Feeling lost and jittery, he watched a group of three of the men cross the street from the building and go into a bar. A couple of others came out, and another went in, shouting something about wife-beaters over his shoulder. That was where they hung out, and that might be a good place to try, if he was going to get anything done. Didn't have wide-open lights in bars, and his sunglasses were big. Maybe he could hear them talking, find out something more before he dared tell anyone how sorry he was to be named Charlie Bell.

When he began to walk again, he saw the bar was called Nick's Hut, and the long window, half sheltered by an overhanging awning, was nearly opaque with grime. Without waiting at the door to give himself a chance to flutter, he went in, made straight for the bar, and leaned against it, holding one hand on top of his head to make sure his cap was still there. The room was divided in two down the middle by a dark-stained wooden partition, but it had so many archways that it was scarcely a partition at all. The rows of booths were high-backed, the lights many-colored, the floor cluttered with old, old sawdust; and the rancid odor of cheap cigars hung from the low ceiling in shreds like crepe paper. The bartender brought him a glass of beer.

The air was stirred only now and then by the sweep of an electric fan perched on a shelf behind a stack of whisky bottles. Charlie watched it for what seemed a long time before he dared to look at any faces. But after the foam had settled on his beer and he'd drunk half, he let his eyes slide to the left of his sunglasses, and he peered through the bleary light at the two men nearest him. They didn't look like anyone. Neither wore a hat, and one had his dirty white shirt unbuttoned all the way down to his belt. He glanced past them, but couldn't see very far toward the back of the room.

Although no one had hollered when he walked in, grabbed him by the shirt, or tried to hit him, he still felt that they all knew who he was. Standing against the bar with the rail pressing a sore place on his shin, he felt spotlighted and caught. He kept trying to tell himself it wasn't true, that he didn't look like the man in the picture now, that they were too crazy to notice him anyway. It worked fairly well. He finished his glass of beer, had it filled up, and started walking down one of the narrow aisles with his head low. Had to find somebody who'd help him. Had to. The whole trip downtown was silly if he couldn't do the only thing that might save him when he got here. Keeping his elbows in so the beer wouldn't get jostled out of his hand, he trudged back the aisle with his eye on a table full of the sort of men he'd seen outside. The booths began behind them, and the first one was empty. He sat down in it, facing front, his face feeling wrinkled and parched with trying to draw it in, shrink it different. He put his glass of beer before him, cupped his chin in his palms, and listened.

There was a lot of racket in the bar, and the juke-box was plunking away at something hillbilly, but now and then during a lull, he could hear the men talking beyond his booth. They spoke mostly about horses, and one of them kept cursing a "Major Charlie."

At first, Charlie was frightened, because he thought they meant him, had somehow confused him with a railroad executive he knew who'd had gold leaves put on his shirt during a rail strike. But when they began arguing about odds, he figured the Major must be just another horse. That Charlie had lost his race. It didn't sound like good luck, and he remembered hearing long ago that when a horse had broken its legs, it was shot. Or was it put to stud? Well, he was almost dead already, and no good at the other any more.

Then, while the juke-box was changing its record, he heard a large, mellow voice say, "Anything new about Lily?"

Another voice said, "Guess not. I just come from the city room. They're going to rehash some of those smears she did on the county machine."

The first man grunted. "How big they going to play her death?"

"Pretty big, I figure. They put old Cracker-Head on rewrite."

Somebody dropped a tray of glasses, and Charlie couldn't hear for a few seconds. He bent further forward, straining.

A different voice said, "She seemed like a pretty good joe. I met her a couple times on the North Side. Shame."

The first man's voice grew more harsh. "Dirty shame."

Charlie felt the moisture from his glass trickle over his fingers.

A new voice, little and thin, said, "She was all right for a dame, but they chuck theirselves around too far sometimes. Don't even know guys like this crossing-jerk are alive. Then first thing they know, they got their brassières tore off and their heads cracked."

Charlie huddled in the booth, jittery with the noise of people he couldn't see, and he remembered a couple of things he'd heard on the record when it was playing in the record shop. The two men had talked of a Senator. Were going to dish his plans for something, and maybe these reporters, or whatever they were, knew enough to guess at. Maybe they'd know what the record meant.

But how could he get them to hear it? They thought he'd done something bad to Lily, then killed her. He sipped his beer. Well, he could just send it to the newspaper, wrap it up in cardboard and send it; but that wouldn't do him any good. They might play it, catch on to what it was all about, and then go roaring off on a news story. He'd still be trying to duck the police, no further along. No, he had to keep it and make someone listen while he still had it. That way, they might possibly believe the rest of his story.

A waitress came by, looked at him, looked at his glass, and went on. He crouched, waiting for something bad to happen, expecting it. He'd been lucky so far, but he wasn't getting any place for the chances he was taking. How to get them to hear the record without losing it?

He couldn't stay any longer, asking them to recognize him and call the police. Had to get outside for a while so he could think of something else. He got up and started down the aisle toward the front. As he passed the table he'd been listening to, he didn't look at the men or say anything, but he wanted to sit down with them and blurt it in their faces, shock them into helping him. He walked past, seeing the smeared light over the aisle grow so thick and bumpy that he didn't think he could wade through it and come to anything clear.

Stopping halfway along the partition beside a tilting stack of empty beer cases, he leaned there, finally realizing that no one was watching him, no one was interested. His head felt funnier than his legs, and when the man in a soiled gray suit stepped by him, put down a suitcase in front of the juke-box, and opened the big glass front with a key, he didn't know at first what the man was doing.

Charlie fingered the long brim of his cap, wishing he could pull it down over his face like a hood and go to sleep. He listened to the noisy record come to an end, and then he saw the man open his suitcase: it was full of records.

In a daze, he went to a vacant part of the bar and got a pick-led pig's foot on a sheet of newspaper, only half knowing he was very hungry. He ate it with his fingers and kept his jacket hitched around in the crook of his elbow, and he watched the man begin to change the selections in the box. He had unplugged the machine, stopped all the circling lights in it, and had started to pull out records from the horizontal row inside. He had some kind of a list on a paper pad in his hand, and he checked things on it with a pencil stub, licking the point and frowning up his small, round face.

Charlie stood by his side and looked closer. All those records.

The man glanced up. "You can play it in a couple minutes. Keep your shirt on."

Without answering, Charlie stood there, his fingers slippery on the clustered bones of the pig's foot. He didn't even know he was eating it. Why couldn't he slip his record in among the others somehow, get it into the new row in the juke-box, then play it right out loud so the whole place could hear? He could watch the reporters while it was going, see how they took it. If it didn't mean anything, it wouldn't be any use to him afterwards, and he could just get out. If they took it big and got excited, he could shove one of the men aside and talk to him, take that big chance.

He wadded the sheet of newspaper around the remains of the pig's foot and wiped his hands on the outside. After he'd wedged it down into an empty beer case, he felt in his jacket pocket for the outline of his record. Again, it was littler than any of those in the machine, but it mightn't make any difference. Maybe nobody'd take notice.

Pinching his mouth back till it looked like someone else's, Charlie tapped the man on the shoulder. "You putting any good ones in?"

The man laughed harshly. "Hell no. There's no money in good ones. These is the worst I could find." He held up one record. "I wouldn't listen to this if I got paid. I bet it gets run every five minutes for the next week."

Charlie looked at it, but the label was turned upside down. He tried to think of some way to make the man leave for a minute, and he began to ease the record out of his jacket pocket. "How's that thing work anyway? Always wondered."

"I don't know." He flicked a long series of little levers.

Desperately, Charlie thought. He had the record all the way out now, holding it carefully down at his side to keep the paper from rattling. "Say, one of the boxes in a booth back there don't work. I dropped in a nickel and nothing happened."

"Which one?"

Charlie pointed through the smoke and the cones of ceiling light. "Third on the right."

The man looked in that direction, then went back to work. "The hell with it. I'll fix it up later, maybe."

"I heard a couple of guys complaining about it. They were kind of sore."

Standing up and scratching his thigh, the man said, "Hell, I'll go tape it shut." He started to walk down the aisle.

Quickly, Charlie stooped and tore the paper off the record. He knew he couldn't get it into the right place in the machine, so he slipped it into the middle of the new stack on the floor. Maybe the man would put it in without looking. As he was evening the records up again, he glanced down the aisle to make sure the man wasn't watching. But he was.

He stood facing the juke-box and staring straight at Charlie. "Which booth did—" He stopped, his eyes widened, and he hurried forward and grabbed Charlie by the arm. "What's going on? You trying to swipe something?"

"No, no. I was just looking."

"Like hell. I seen you messing around." He tightened his hand hard on Charlie's arm.

A bartender in a white apron came around the bar, circled a couple of men who were laughing together, and came over to the black, open suitcase. "What's the trouble, Frankie?"

The juke-box man said, "This joker was trying to hook some of my records. I oughta slug him."

Charlie said, "It's all a mistake. Nothing happened." He tried to tug his arm away, but he couldn't. Had to keep this from getting worse, had to get away now in a hurry.

The bartender put his hands on his hips. "Who'd want to steal any of them dumb things? You must be cracking up, Frankie."

The juke-box man said, "I got enough troubles without stumble-bums like this nosing in my stuff. I guess he thinks he's a engineer or something."

The bartender said, "Forget it." He turned to Charlie. "Just go somewhere else, bud."

"Sure." Charlie looked down at the floor where his record was, and didn't know what to do. Couldn't just leave it. It might still help him.

The man let go of his arm and, muttering to himself, began fumbling in the machine again. The bartender walked away.

Stooping as fast as he could without hurting his legs, Charlie got his fingers into the right niche and pulled out his record. He was just turning to duck out as quietly as possible, when the juke-box man grabbed him again and shoved him.

The man said, "Christ, what's up with you? I got to bean you or something?"

Charlie felt himself spin and stagger, and he rammed his shoulder against the empty beer cases. His cap fell off and landed on the floor, and one temple of his glasses came unhooked so that they dangled down across his mouth. Recovering slowly, still hanging onto the record, he reached down for his cap and picked it out of a layer of sawdust. He felt afraid of his sudden nakedness, and for a stretched-out few seconds, he gaped toward the front, along the bar, at all the faces turned his way. One man stepped apart from the others, looking amazed, and Charlie recognized the stocky man who'd jumped off the train, who'd hit him before, who'd probably killed Lily.

The juke-box man said, "Give me that thing back."

Jamming his cap on, Charlie turned and walked fast toward the back of the room. The man was still hollering about the record, and he caught Charlie by his shirt collar, whirled him around, and swung at him, grazing his jaw. Then the bartender was between them, both arms held out stiff, trying to thrust them apart, and the juke-box man swung again, hitting the bartender on the shoulder. With his mouth open, Charlie backed away, and he saw the stocky man coming down the aisle, turning sideways to get by the two men who had just started to argue loudly. Pushed by the juke-box man, the bartender staggered backward and clamped the stocky man against the bar. He shoved in return. Then a lot of shoving started.

Charlie headed for the rear. Every angle of the walls, the ceiling, and the booths was muddied and distorted because his sunglasses only covered one eye, and he didn't have time or the free hand to get them straight. He went as quickly as he could, dodging between men who were standing in the aisle, weaving in and out of the oddly spaced doors in the central partition. Once he looked back and thought he saw the stocky man following, but because he used his one dark eye, he couldn't really be sure.

In the vague part of his mind, he'd been hoping there'd be a rear door to help him pull a sneak, but when he came even with the last few booths where only a couple of old men sat, he saw just a wooden wall and some streaked cardboard beer ads. Behind him, he heard someone knock over a chair, and he took the only other way: into the men's room. There, panicked so that the muscles over his heart jumped and twitched, he pulled the door shut and slid an old bolt into place, having to punch at it with the side of his hand because it had been painted over.

The door began to jiggle immediately, and someone wrenched at the knob so hard that the inside half fell off and rolled on the floor. Trembling, he put the record back in his jacket pocket, took off his glasses, and looked around. Have to try a window.

An old man with his dirty white shirt-tail hanging down the back of his pants stood wavering at the edge of the urinal, and he looked over his shoulder at Charlie. The man's face was bright red, and a trickle of saliva came down the corner of his mouth. He grinned. "They gonna get you?" He braced himself with one hand against the wall. "I ain't got no money either."

Shoving his glasses into his pocket, Charlie pushed with all his might at the handles of a chest-high window on the far side of the john.

The old man said, "That don't never work."

The window opened grudgingly a foot and a half and stopped dead. He reached through it, took hold of the outside ledge, and using a short radiator as a stair, got the upper part of his body out into the dark. Because the window was too narrow, he couldn't swing his legs around now and get them down first, so he had to throw his jacket to the ground and hold fast to the window-sash while he wiggled through to one side. Finally, his legs came free as he clung, bracing one elbow on the ledge, and he let them drop as gently as he could to the gravel.

In a high, croaking voice, the old man said, "Good-by."

Charlie picked up his jacket and groped his way over a slanting lot pocketed with gullies and filled with small sheds. In the blackness, he bumped into the warped weatherboards that were bowed away from the corners of the sheds, and often the splinters ran through his shirtsleeves and scraped his arms. Maybe the stocky man would tell everyone in the bar who he was, remind them what he had done, and perhaps soon they'd come poking flashlights and shouting, forcing him to run through this rubble and lose his mind.

He cracked his left knee against the edge of an overturned oil drum, and the pain nearly made him cry out. As he limped on, he tied the sleeves of his jacket around his waist like an apron and let the front drape his legs.

After the last shed, he came to a curving alley whose ruts were inlaid with jagged stone, and even though it led slightly uphill and would be hard to manage, he took it, trying to keep in the middle, trying to listen above the scuffling of his safety shoes. He couldn't hear anyone behind him, but he didn't let himself depend on that. Might be like the night before: a sign they were after you the most.

The alley led, heaving and knotting itself, to a side street west of the tavern. He stood at the mouth and didn't know what way to pick. The alley didn't continue on the other side of the street, and it was dead-end behind him at the river. He turned left, away from Madison and the *Evening News*, and hurried down the sidewalk past frame buildings where the paint peeled down to lie on the pavement and be drifted into the gutters along with paper and dust. The streetlights were far away, dimmer than moonlight. Untying his jacket and pulling his cap further down, he limped toward the next corner, clenching his teeth against each jolt.

Once there, he stopped to rest, leaning his shoulder against a tall tin sign beside a covered wooden stairway at the front of a building. The sign had contained a thermometer, but the glass tube had been broken out and the enamel lettering chipped off. He looked back along the street.

Three or four men came running around the corner of Madison and hurried down the sidewalk toward him. He stepped back into the opening at the foot of the stairway and peeked past the shattered jamb in their direction. They turned into the alley he'd just left. But more men were coming behind them, and some of them didn't turn. He pulled his head in and wearily began to climb the dark stairs.

He was exhausted before he reached the first landing, and when he lifted his feet for the last few steps, his toes kept catching at the worn rubber stair-pads. He felt in the dark for a doorknob, found it, and the door was locked. He wasn't surprised. He sat down on the top step and waited.

But it wasn't like resting. The noise of running from right to left went past the foot of the stairs, then more running, then silence, then running from left to right. Nobody came up. Everything he tried to do got busted, twisted somehow, and he could see it wasn't going to be any good just keeping away from trains. They weren't the only things that had it in for him. All kinds of people could huff and shoot smoke, break up the inside of his head till it rattled. And now he didn't even know what time it was any more. No place to be, to lie down, and he knew if he ever did get a chance to relax in calm, clean air, he'd be able to smell his own feet.

After a long wait, during which there was no more noise, he went down the stairs and stood in the half light just inside the doorway. Still no sound. Cautiously he put his head out and looked both ways. Nobody. Tightening the muscles of his stomach, he forced himself to leave the alcove and crossed the street to the other side, even though the dim streetlight would show him to anyone standing near the corner of the *Evening News*. He walked into the shadows of another frame building, safe out of sight from everyone but himself. He stared at his feet as he limped on them, and he felt certain there was nothing inside his shoes. Maybe just a pair of old socks, but no feet. He couldn't feel them, and every step was like sinking into a featherbed up to his knees. Wasn't any way to go except down a few blocks, then double back north through busy streets. Couldn't stay and hide there. No, maybe south toward Union Station, around it, out of it. Somewhere darker, slower.

A car turned the corner a block ahead of him and came down his street slowly, spraying its spotlights out to either side. He backed up to a grocery he'd just passed, edged into its doorway, and opened the screen door to step in. Then he stood facing the glass of the inside door, nose to nose with his own shadowy reflection, toeing his feet out in the narrow space, and he let the screen door swing nearly shut against his back. The car went by, dazzling him momentarily with a sweep of light. It didn't stop.

For a while he let himself go, staring at the dark hollows in the glass, an inch away, where his eyes should be. He couldn't see them. The greasy surface was cold against his nose, and his ankles began to hurt from standing splayfooted. Then after another minute, he pushed gently on the screen door with his behind, turned, and looked both ways on the street. Deserted again. Well, every once in a while it was. He started walking, and walking made him light-headed and took away all sense of what was real. After he'd gone by, he remembered passing patched-together wrecks of houses where not a light showed, weedy lots, a boarded-up drugstore, but his mind always lagged behind and didn't register them as he saw them. It was a good way to keep from being afraid, because he didn't notice momentary dangers like too much light, a man on the other side of the street, a cruising taxi, till they were already past. Then it was too late to worry. Like having insurance that paid off every minute.

Two blocks later, when his knees began to buckle out of rhythm, he turned right and headed back toward Madison Street. He put on his dark glasses again because he saw the lights of a dozen dumpy taverns ahead, and he wanted to keep himself from seeing anything too frightening. The rummies stood in clusters on the grassless strip between curb and sidewalk, or they flopped in doorways and slept. One was even lying in the middle of the street, groaning. No one looked at him or helped.

Charlie knew he probably looked like one of them by this time, but he kept his head straight and his mouth shut. And when he found himself walking slower and slower over the glass-strewn sidewalk, at first he didn't know why. He took a deeper breath to see whether the air was thicker than before, whether it had turned into water or mud. He came to a full stop and still didn't know why. He stared ahead, and finally he realized he was seeing policemen. There were two of them at the fully lighted corner, half a block away, and they were asking the rummies questions, bending to look at the faces of those who were lying down or sitting slumped over. And they were working their way down the sidewalk toward him.

Wearily, he turned to the nearest rummy, a man sitting with his back against the bricks of a tavern-side, hands and head between his knees.

In a dull voice, Charlie said, "You want a drink?" And he reached down and began helping the man to his feet.

The man said, "Uh." His blue coat-sleeves came only halfway between elbow and wrist.

Although the pain was lancing all the way up into his thighs, Charlie heaved the man upright, pulled one limp arm around his own neck, and reached around the man's back to support him under the further armpit. "I'll buy you a drink."

They staggered forward, the man's toes sometimes dragging, sometimes taking steps, toward the policemen. He didn't think.

One of the cops stood in their way, stopping them, and he put his night-stick under the rummy's chin, lifted it till his head lolled back, took a good look, and let it drop. Charlie waited to get hit, waited to begin giving up, but the policeman went away, so he started for the corner again, his eyes only half open behind his glasses.

The policemen were shifting around, crossing the side street off Madison, going deeper into the shadows he'd left behind. One of them said, "What's he supposed to look like again?"

Where the ten-foot side window of the tavern began, Charlie let the man sit down on the sidewalk, easing him back till his head rested against a rain-streaked snuff ad. He got a dollar out of his pocket and put it inside the man's shirt, not even caring if somebody saw him.

When he took the three steps to the corner, he peered around the bare shoulder of a man in a dirty undershirt and nosed his glasses down to look along the street toward Nick's Hut, even though it didn't really matter. He didn't see the stocky man, and that was enough for now. Waiting to let a rumbling streetcar pass, he crossed to the other side and went into the dark again, not lifting his shoes high enough to keep the heels from scraping and not caring. His legs could go to hell.

Long afterward, he remembered thinking maybe they'd done just that. He wasn't walking any more. He was floating over the torn-up, tilted sidewalk without a single light to look at. No clocks. He felt thin as a piece of scrap paper, edging its way through slits where streets should have been. And his head turned like a record or a wheel oozing oil and dead steam. Single tracks, straight and rusty under him. He turned a few corners and came back into light and noise, but they soon disappeared again.

And then, blocks later, he bumped into an old woman, and her swearing woke him up. He was nearing a wide street that was busy with cars, and off to the right was an immense building. He didn't have to read the faint neon letters around the top to know it was the Union Station. Trains born in there. He waited for a few seconds, making his mind blink itself sharper; then he crossed toward it over the cracking asphalt, not interested in whether a car hit him or not. Maybe he could take a train somewhere, keep himself moving. It was all the last few days needed to make them complete. He supposed he should die on a train, after all that had happened. Have everything come out in two circles: from birth, to the freights that fell on you, to murder, then running in a circle, and coming back to be killed. Figure eight. He got one foot on the first broad, flat step to an entrance, but he couldn't bring the other up beside it. He stood there and took off his glasses for last looks.

Someone was running down the sidewalk at the far end of the building, running clumsily and not very fast. He watched the man and noticed that he had no suitcase, that he was short and husky, but he didn't pay any more heed to those things than he did to the way the single headlight of a taxi, knocked awry, flashed light crazily along all the windows on a building opposite him. He got his legs to move him up the stairs toward the door, yet he didn't hurry, couldn't. A young, perspiring woman, who was carrying a boston bag and a little boy, nudged past him and backed into the entrance, using her bottom as a pusher. Charlie followed her, wondering where he was and what he was doing, and he entered the first big waiting room with its anchored, pew-like benches and imitation marble walls that stretched up out of his sight. As he took the last of the inside steps carefully and methodically, he put on his glasses again. People were looking at him. A coiled-up, tow-headed buck private stopped snoring when Charlie passed and followed him with puffed eyes. Two old women, stifling in thick clothes, gaped dully in silence at the way he limped. Tugging the brim of his cap, he began to think again and worry.

He shuffled to the first broad aisle where a neon arrow pointed left in the direction of the trains, and only then did he remember to look back to the entrance. The stocky man was there, of course. No longer running, but walking quickly past the benches. He looked straight at Charlie and held his mouth open to gasp and cough. Charlie felt that the man would always be following him, from now till death on a train, and maybe he would never quite get caught. He felt a little sorry for the man who had nothing better to do than run in the middle of June.

Trying to get rid of his grogginess by rubbing the back of his neck, Charlie turned the corner and edged through a group of Girl Scouts to an open space along the ticket windows. The woman who was leading the Scouts glared at him and started to come back to say something, but she didn't. She hurried the girls along, using the flat of her hand on each one's back. He walked at their side till he couldn't listen to their giggling whispers any more; then he turned off between high rows of package lockers that led right from the main causeway in a short U. There, out of sight at the base, he stopped and made himself breathe more slowly. The sweat ran down the insides of his arms.

Have to take a train somewhere, after letting the stocky man get confused for a while longer. Where? Just the first train. Someone might recognize him, but conductors, trainmen, and passengers were only people, not like these others, not like police. He'd go somewhere and die. Maybe even die before he got there.

He hadn't felt this bad since his accident. Seemed like a long time. A long time to worry about how to stand, walk, go up and down steps. And such a long time forgetting what you couldn't forget.

And he didn't want to think about it, not now, but it came anyway. It came as the freight car had come. He remembered standing in the snow that evening beside the frozen switch, holding the stiff switch-broom in his hands, looking at the way the red and green lights splotched his pants. The chisel-end of the broom hadn't budged the mechanism, but fire had done the trick, finally, and he had stood at the edge of the icy frog then, seeing the shadowed engine on the far side of the slope budge the empty freezer-car to the hump and let it go. And through the falling snow and the near-dark he had seen the freezer coming toward the switch, almost silent, not very fast, and at the last moment he had noticed what he should have seen before, what he was damned for not seeing: just beyond the glow of the switch lights, the dim outline of a tie placed crosswise over the tracks by kids or someone. And the freezer, close to him now and huge, had hit the tie and tilted slowly over him, its side door wide open like a mouth; and he'd only had time to fall down in the snow before the car derailed and tipped over sideways to box all of him except his legs in the frame of the open door. Like a mouse under a hat. And when he could finally sit up in the dark, he had been inside the freezer and could reach forward and knock on the floor with the switch-broom, and could feel the top of the doorjamb just below his kneecaps, and could tell no difference between his legs and the mushy snow under and between them.

Well, at least there was no way to remember exactly how things hurt. You could forget that. But he felt himself shaking, his hands against the locker doors. The air didn't move around him, and his nose was clogging with the same breaths he'd taken a few seconds before. Surely the stocky man must have gone by, started into the main waiting room, or ducked back to watch another exit by this time. Had to get something else to eat: the pig's foot was knotting his stomach and making the top of his throat taste greasy. Had to move, sleep, get away, find out everything in the world about Lily, die.

When the fat old lady waddled into the aisle of lockers, pushing a red cardboard suitcase in front of her with her feet, and began jabbering at a dark, meek little man behind her, Charlie knew he'd have to get out or be plungered out by her like something caught in a drain. He went slowly to the other mouth of the U and waited there, watching everyone who went by. The steady stream in both directions was mostly soldiers and sailors, hunched under dufflebags and satchels; those leaving the main waiting room were streaked with sleep and dust, those entering either fresh, clean and laughing, or drunk. All eyes were empty.

He was out among them before he'd made up his mind to take the chance. He followed the jostling traffic into the main room, keeping his head pulled in and his shoulders lower than anyone else. His dark glasses slowed down the bustle a lot, made it less painful, but the people all appeared vicious to him. He knew he wouldn't be able to stand seeing them fight among themselves and snarl to get on the trains first, and he wished his glasses were darker, even black. The heat of their bodies packed the room like wadding, and by the time he'd wormed his way through to the straggling cluster around the gateway to an eastbound train, his shirt was wet and his jacket felt as though it were burning over his arm.

Five soldiers were shooting a quiet game of crap against a stack of luggage in the middle of the crowd, and they squatted on their haunches, mumbling, throwing down five-dollar bills. Charlie stood behind the fattest man he could see, one whose summer suitcoat was beginning to split up the back seam, and he watched the game from around the man's thick neck. He felt protected there, safe, because he stood between the fat man and the shut gate to the train. The people nearby kept their eyes on the dice, not on him.

The fat man said, "Little Joe from Kokomo," and he chuckled.

The man's body was like a big sack full of heat, and Charlie felt himself being lulled by it, drained of all effort to stay awake. He heard the dice clatter against an upright suitcase, but he couldn't see them any more. His eyes kept closing, and even when he opened them again, he saw only the inside of his glasses. Leaning against the wooden door, he let himself doze. Wouldn't dare sit down. Sitting duck. Gut the Senator, plug us. Who was the Senator? The old woman from Tyrone, Pennsylvania, would probably never find the Friday House, Farraday House. There was a convention in a week or so, something with politics. Lily would know, did know. The record knew, but wouldn't say. Somebody grabbed him by the arm and wrenched his glasses off. They gouged both his ears.

He opened his eyes and saw the stocky man. It was all over for a while.

The man pinned him to the door, pressing his elbow against Charlie's chest, and said, "All right, Bell, hand the stuff over and there won't be no trouble."

Charlie smiled and nodded, but he didn't do anything.

Keeping his voice low and flat, the stocky man said, "I don't want to get rough. You seen what happened to her."

Charlie was very embarrassed at actually meeting this man, and he didn't know how to act. The man had too many creases in his face, too much red. His buggy eyes were too close together. He just wanted to keep away from him, away from the violence and the stink of murder.

The man said, "One more chance, wise guy. I'll fan you right here and leave you for the cops."

Charlie nodded again, not knowing why.

Someone with a deep, croaking voice said, "Come on, bust it up. What's the idea?"

Startled, the stocky man turned to look. A broad, sleek-faced MP was nudging the crap game apart, his billy-club prodding the soldiers in the ribs.

Taking one step sideways along the door, Charlie brought his right arm back and sloshed the stocky man in the neck with the edge of his hand. He staggered and almost fell, but he kept hold of Charlie's shirt. He said, "God damn it."

The fat man in the summer suit said, "What's the trouble?"

Gently, Charlie tried to loosen the fingers that were nearly tearing his shirt-front.

The stocky man said, "Try that again, Bell, and I'll *really* put you away." He drew Charlie close to him and glared in his eyes.

The fat man said, "Let go of him."

Turning his head slowly, the stocky man looked at the other for a moment. He said, "Shut up."

Charlie agreed. He was quite ready to give in. Maybe he could get himself killed and be done with it.

The fat man said, "Well, I didn't have anything to do anyway," and he stepped behind the stocky man, grabbed the bottom of his suit-coat, and yanked it upwards till it snarled, inside out, at the armpits. The stocky man let go of Charlie, turned, kneed the fat man in the stomach, and drew back his fist to hit him.

Charlie quit watching and walked away, sorry to start again. He took his time, partly because one foot had gone to sleep and partly because he didn't want anyone in the waiting room to take a second look at him, now that his glasses were gone. Two languid Chinese girls, with skirts split up to their knees, chattered at him when he bumped into them, but he kept going till the crowd thinned near the information desk. He started through the same doorway he'd entered by, and when he looked back, he saw the stocky man charging in his direction, head down, ramming his shoulders into old ladies and redcaps. Couldn't hurt the man, but it felt good to hit him. Making up a little for the lobster bin, the broken watch. Keeping next to the wall in the causeway, he limped against the traffic to the entrance of the locker section where he'd hidden before. He slipped into it and went around the first bend.

He knew it wouldn't work again, not the same thing. The stocky man would look there, find him, maybe kill him. The big woman with the red suitcase was gone, so he couldn't even use her as a blockade. Well, perhaps if he just left the record and the pictures of checks here on the floor, the stocky man would find them and go away. But he wanted to keep them. If people needed them so badly, they might get him out of all the mess. His hands and legs were shaking, trying to come apart, to fail him altogether.

Without really thinking, he sat on the floor and opened one of the big quarter lockers that still had a key in it. Big enough, some place dark. He lifted his feet in and slid them back along the metal bottom, then scrunched forward till they touched the back. By bending his knees up, he got his whole body inside, the seat of his pants almost against his heels, and when he let his head lie back and eased the door shut with his hand, it rested against the top of his cap and stayed ajar only an inch. Then he folded his arms over his chest and waited.

It was just like going away somewhere. Nobody else was here. The lip of the door caught a draft and kept the air from getting too stale, and his legs, though bent sharply at the knees, relaxed for the first time in many hours. Nice to be way inside something where you didn't have to see or be. A pair of shoes went clicking by on the hard floor, but he didn't get afraid, hold his breath, swallow to keep his heart down. Didn't have to. Nothing to be afraid of.

The walls and ceiling of the locker touched him, then touched him more firmly, softly. He didn't try to stay awake, because he was already nowhere and you couldn't go anywhere from nowhere. He said good-by in the dark; and as his mind slid away backward, he heard the faraway steam-whistle of the train that was about to come down the square tunnel toward him, pistons racketing through their oil, bell throwing its clapper into the black smoke. It would run over him.

CHAPTER SIX

With one foot on the floor and one foot still between the sheets, Senator Taggart lay on the bed and thought about getting up. Sometimes he thought he would, and sometimes he thought he wouldn't. The featureless ceiling was not in the least designed to hold his interest, but then there was always the alternative of closing his eyes and not looking at anything. He mused.

A breeze with no backbone filtered through the screen of the bedroom window, making the hanging edge of the sheet sway back and forth and tickle his leg. He sat up and held his head. Somewhere beneath the heavy mat of hair he knew there was a skull, but it now felt the size of a walnut. Or a medium-large ball-bearing. The main difficulty in pretending to run for President was that you had to give too many parties, and you never escaped without toasting yourself at least twenty times. Experimentally, he stood up, teetered back so far that he had to reach around and shove at the mattress, righted himself, and walked toward the bathroom. The apparition in the mirror above the dresser startled him, and he nearly turned back to the bed. No, every day had to start sometime.

He picked up his watch and put it down. Eight-thirty. The things a man was forced to do. Letting his pajamas fall here and there, he stepped into the shower, braced himself by holding onto the cold-water handle, and turned on the hot. He didn't sing.

The door to the dining room opened, and Fred Hax said, "Some phone calls."

The Senator pretended not to hear. He let the water coast down his back and reached for the soap.

Fred said, "One from your boy in Chicago."

The Senator pondered for a moment. "Which boy?"

"Hindruth."

"All right. I'll get it in a minute." The trouble was people kept bringing up details, kept asking about them. Simplest thing in the world to operate with a grand scope if people would just shut up about details. Every unpleasant person he'd ever known had always been fascinated by details. So picayune.

He dried himself, put on a voluminous terry-cloth bathrobe, and went into the dining room. Fred Hax was eating scrambled eggs and flicking over the pages of a memorandum book.

The Senator said, "What's he want?"

Fred pushed the floor buzzer with his foot and said, "I don't know. But he's stewing about something."

"Everybody's always stewing. I wish I knew some serene people." He started for the front room and the telephone, but stopped when the cook stuck her head through the swinging door to the kitchen. He pointed at Fred's plate. "Same for me, only double. And moisten the orange juice with something. I've got a head."

"Yes, Senator."

The pad beside the telephone told him the number of some operator to call, but he didn't feel like reading. He dialed long-distance. "This is Senator Taggart. Chicago call for me?" He yawned steadily for a minute while the phone clicked, sputtered, and murmured.

A voice said, "That you, Phil?"

"Is this Hindruth?"

"Yes."

The Senator reached for a cigarette, licked his teeth and lips, and changed his mind. "What's the fuss?"

"I've been trying to get you since last night."

Hindruth's voice was high-pitched, fluty, and the Senator held the receiver several inches further from his ear. "I was out. And I don't take calls when I'm asleep."

Hindruth said, "Look, there's kind of a mess here. We need your help right away."

"Well, what is it?"

"A woman from the honest newspaper—you know?—swiped some of the briefcase material from Cooper. And we think some railroad crossing watchman has it. The reporter got herself—is no longer with us."

The Senator looked at the telephone. "Is that supposed to make sense?"

A thin laugh came from the other end of the wire. "Sorry, Phil. I didn't get any sleep. Been trying to call you. It's all mixed up in my mind."

The Senator thought about hanging up, but it would have taken too much effort. He waited.

"How freely can I talk? I'm not very good at this."

"Nobody taps this wire. Now start over again, will you?"

"The police think the watchman killed the reporter, see, and he's running around town somewhere with the record of Corrigan making that deal and some of the Bergnauer checks. You don't want them let out, do you?"

"No."

"Then you'd better start making some phone calls. I don't know how to handle it."

The Senator sighed. "I'll think about it. Anything else?"

After a pause, Hindruth said, "Well, I don't know, but I think maybe one of us may get in trouble over the killing."

"What makes you think so?"

Hindruth sniffed a few times and said, "It's pretty complicated."

"Spare me. I'll find out about it somehow." Then although he didn't really care particularly, he said, "How are things going?"

Hindruth's voice got even louder. "How does it sound like they're going, for God's sake? I'm waiting for things to collapse any minute, and I don't like it, Phil."

The Senator could feel his face getting hot. "Listen, don't ever shout at me, especially in the morning. I mean it. Or I'll send you back to bookkeeping."

"Sorry, Phil. I think I'd like to go back to the books. How am I going to face Corrigan and Bergnauer this morning with these things floating around loose? I'm seeing Corrigan in an hour and a half."

With his fingers impatiently twiddling the connection-break button, the Senator said, "Just go ahead and do it. That's how. And go around to your office when you're done. There'll be somebody to see you."

"Who?"

"Never mind. Just be there. Anything else?" After listening to the long silence, the Senator said, "You're feeling pretty free with your money, dawdling around on a call like this."

Hindruth said, "I called collect. Didn't Fred tell you? I don't have much money left, now that you mention it."

"Pretend I didn't. I'm hanging up."

"Phil?"

"Yes."

Hindruth paused again. "Those two men, Cooper and the other one, they're not very savory characters."

"I didn't ask you to eat them." The Senator put the receiver back in its cradle and wanted to shake his head sadly, but instead, he put one hand on top of it and went into the dining room.

Fred put down his coffee cup. "Anything that matters?"

He sat down, and the cook put eggs in front of him. "Go out and get me a Chicago paper. The *Evening News* preferably."

Fred finished his coffee and left.

It was all very well to play around with electioneering just to see or hear your name tossed hither and yon and maybe to pick up enough delegates to be worthy of favors from some of the really big boys, but you couldn't let it get too far out of hand. Couldn't let it get messy. It had to be kept a good, clean, expensive sport that left you with a trifle more power and a few more people knowing your name. You could even wind up with more money than you started with sometimes, but that wasn't important. Perhaps the blackmail had been a mistake, a little on the sloppy side. But it was all in the game, even if you weren't playing for keeps.

And the hitch was that the ones who were backing you or following you or rallying around you got so serious. And you could never let them know you weren't. The need for pretense took away most of the fun.

He drank his orange juice and made a mental note to tell the cook that brandy wasn't quite right for mornings. The eggs looked despondent. He ate them, letting his mind go fuzzy.

Just as he finished, Fred brought in the paper and put it on the table. "It's yesterday afternoon's." Then he stood around for a while, read off a list of appointments, spoke knowingly about the stock market, and went into the front room.

The Senator looked at the front page and read the story about Lily Gonchar and Charles Bell slowly. There was no mention of any record or checks. How did Hindruth know who had them? For that matter, how did Hindruth know anything about anything? The story didn't make any more sense than the phone call.

He went into the other room. "Get Bob Quiller on the phone. He got into Chicago this morning. I mean, he was supposed to. Try the Blackstone."

Fred got up from the sofa. "What do you want me to tell him?"

"Nothing. I'll talk to him. *Somebody's* got to find out what the hell is going on in that town. Hindruth's out of his head."

Fred nodded and picked up the receiver.

The Senator went to the window and held the newspaper in the sunshine. The only thing the least bit political about the story was the woman. He remembered being shown a couple of things she'd written. A bitch of the first water. He held the paper at arm's length and squinted at the picture of Bell. Looked familiar, but then most faces were beginning to look familiar. This one was about a ninth-row face, back where the squirming started earliest. The kind that didn't change the look-what-you-did-to-me-last-time expression no matter what a speech said. Well, people got into the damnedest kinds of trouble, and it was mostly because they didn't have large plans. Always wading around in details. He looked at the picture again, yawned, and put the paper down. The kind of face it was best to stare earnestly beyond in a meeting hall, not ever touching eyes. He looked like a voter.

CHAPTER SEVEN

Charlie was waking up anyway, his own coughing and his own smell doing the trick, but when the woman screeched and let the locker door swing back to hit him on top of the head, his eyes came open and stayed open. He knew where he was. No question about remembering, and pushing with his feet, he got his head out into the aisle. At first, the bill of his baseball cap was in the way, and he thought maybe the woman was behind him where he couldn't see. Yet when he tilted the brim and looked, he could tell it was only a little girl, even though she was upside down. He scrabbled out, twisting, till he was on his hands and aching knees.

The little girl had an upturned flowerpot of brown hair, cut in bangs over her eyebrows. Mouth puckered, she stared at him.

Charlie said, "Where's your mommy?"

The little girl just stared, rocking forward on her toes.

He pulled himself to a standing position with the edge of a locker. The girl's mother had probably run to find somebody, spieling headlines: man in a locker, dead. Throat cut from jaw to jaw. He'd have to go away, but he wasn't at all sure he could walk. Avoiding the eyes of the little girl, he went to the bend in the aisle, propping himself hand over hand on the small locker knobs. Well, his legs were ruined for good. He couldn't straighten either of them, and he could feel the burning splotches down the insides of his shins. At the narrow opening to the causeway, he stopped to put on his jacket. Hot or not, he couldn't carry it, and it might make him look different. He turned up the collar.

Feeling lost because he had no idea what time it was, Charlie was frightened at how few people were walking to the main waiting room. He'd be more conspicuous. He might have stood there undecided for ten minutes, taking a rest, but he saw a short, black-haired woman trotting toward the U of lockers, followed by a station agent and a policeman, so he began to shuffle as casually as possible along the causeway in their direction. He tugged at his cap brim.

They passed him without a look and went into the near end of the U, the woman panting and frantic. He watched his feet wading through their own pain, the cramped bow of his legs, the littered floor, and by the time he came to the width and height of the waiting room, he didn't know whether he would finish the next step on his head or on his rear. His lungs were clotted with stale air, choking him, making him cough and yawn at the same time.

Along the right wall were the gates to the trains, a few of them clustered with waiting people. He'd had some idea last night. Yes, to take a train and let it carry him somewhere. But there were so many others who wanted to go away too. Except policemen. They wouldn't go away. Two were standing, large and solid, near the information desk, and another was wandering past the gates, going in the opposite direction. Looking for him?

Nearby, a redcap was trundling a barrow of suitcases through one of the open, otherwise deserted doorways to the tracks. Charlie followed him. He would look like a worker, could even act like one if put to it. And this way there wouldn't be any ticket-checking conductors looking at him right away, and he could take his pick of trains.

But when he wavered through the gate without being stopped, and stood inside for a moment to gain nerve, he didn't gain any nerve at all, for the trains were there, some of them making noise, and thousands of glinting tracks, and ties brown with dust. And he knew he couldn't do it. All the air went out of him, and he stood under the low, blackened ceiling, facing the endless lines of passenger cars like gigantic link-sausages. He was afraid.

He would have to go back inside where there were people. They were bad enough, but not this bad. Keeping his head turned away from the nightmare beside him, he walked unsteadily to a girder-like stanchion, picked up an unlit trainman's lantern by its hoop-handle, turned, and went back through the gate. If anyone noticed or cared, they'd think he was a derelict from a repair crew. But he didn't look at any faces to see what they thought. He wasn't looking for anybody, had nothing to find. He kept his eyes blurred and remembered that railroad men called this kind of lantern a bird cage. Well, there was no bird in it. And no kind of fire. It didn't make anything brighter.

He wandered more or less to the right, past the information desk, taking millions of steps that all seemed too little, into another room, skirting people and benches, and made his way to what he remembered as the dimmest exit. They were probably all watching for him. Even the stocky man, ready to keep up the round-robin.

It came to him as a shock, while he was using the ends of benches as a sporadic handrail, that it might be daylight outside. He didn't have his dark glasses any more, and he'd have to look different or someone would surely recognize him. Not that it mattered much, but he felt obliged to worry about it, keep up the pretense of getting away. No way to stop, really, unless they stopped him.

On the last bench toward another corridor, he saw a penny box of safety matches lying on a newspaper, and because no one sat beside them, he picked them up. He remembered something he'd done long ago. When was it? He put the matches in his pocket, ignoring the newspaper that might tell him horrible new things about himself, and set the lantern on the bench. Somebody would find it there. It wasn't like stealing.

He made the corridor where most of the people were coming his way, and he went along it, keeping his mouth closed. He trudged to the swung-back glass doors and stopped there. The taxicabs blatted their horns on the below-ground-level runway and zoomed to the doorway to let out passengers, but he didn't look at them. He turned to face the glass in one of the doors and lit a match. His yellow-edged reflection was vague, and it died away as the match burned out. Then he leaned close to his own face, and with the stub of the wooden match he charcoaled a thick mustache under his nose and out to the ends of his mouth. He puffed his lips and blew away the excess.

Now he was ready. He had to go to the hammer track for repairs, had to get to a doctor about his legs, or he couldn't go on to prove anything or escape anything. Get patched up, then see. Nobody would expect a mustache on the face they'd seen in the papers, not this soon. He felt better, but he couldn't take the two steps out onto the landing to hail a taxi. Legs quit working. He leaned against the metal rail, hip-high across the door, and squinted under his cap in hopes he could catch a cabby's eye. They'd have to see him sooner or later, and now he could take a little rest.

He waited for a long time, but no one spoke to him or helped him. Maybe he didn't look old enough or rich enough to be worth a hand. Finally, when a cab swung in and let out a man and a noisy woman, he lifted his arm to wave at the cabby and even took the first step away from the door; but the cab driver was gunning the engine and not looking. Legs loose as rubber, Charlie felt himself lunge down the two steps, nearly ramming the woman back into the taxi, and he came to a halt with both arms through the open back window and his legs nowhere. The woman stopped talking long enough to glare at him. After she was out, he inched around the open door and half fell into the back seat, letting his legs trail in by themselves. The door slammed itself, and he shut his eyes.

He said, "Clark and Jackson." And he didn't know why. Just a corner like any other. There'd be a doctor somewhere near. Keeping his eyes shut, he felt the motor whirr in his ears like a clock, nasty, uneven, and he didn't want to see whether the sun was up when the cab came to the top of the runway. No. He went into a jumpy sleep.

The cab driver said, "Here you are, buddy."

They were at the curb, and the door was already open. Fishing in his pocket for money, he eased his feet over the running board to the street and handed the man a dollar. Then he wavered on the curb, the weight of his body pressing hard on his run-down heels, and he saw the sun streaking from the south edge of Jackson along the buildings on the other side. Daytime, and people would be looking at him. He tried to take confidence from his new mustache, and it helped a little. Setting his eyes on the nearest doorway that looked like an office building, he went for it, hearing his toes scrape the pavement with each step.

The small, marble-lined lobby of the building was nearly deserted, and he looked around for a directory. Aside from the single elevator, there was only one door, and through it he saw the high, disordered shelves of a bookstore. Not that way. He found the directory next to the elevator, and because another man was waiting there, he scanned it in a hurry. A chiropodist was listed on the second floor, and feeling pretty sure that a chiropodist had something to do with feet or ankles, he memorized the number. Well, his shins hurt most, but if somebody could fix up feet, they could go a little higher if they had to, probably. Dr. Chandler, 207. He looked wistfully at the stairway, but knew he couldn't manage that.

After several moments the elevator door opened, and Charlie let the other man who was waiting go first. Then he followed and muttered to the operator, "Two." He watched the worn metal rim near his feet.

Though he'd expected the two people in the car to end the party by knowing who he was, neither one did, and he got out at the first stop feeling lucky and near home. This Dr. Chandler might not be fooled, but foot doctors probably paid more attention to feet than to faces. He didn't remember anything in the papers about his feet or his shoes.

Number 207 was at the bend in the musty hallway, the door half open, and he went that way as though tottering to the end of a diving board. He didn't even pause to scout the waiting room first, but entered at a stagger and flopped into the nearest chair. He sat there, clasping both knees, and didn't realize for the time it took to rub his shins gently that he was alone.

The outer office was like a shallow box: shadowy in the corners, plain, smelling of old things. On the far wall was a picture of a skeleton foot: the toes, the arch bones, the beginnings of the ankle named with black letters and little arrows. His own feet felt even less substantial. There were only two chairs and a scratched deal table sloppily cluttered with magazines. He felt so completely closed-in and safe that even when the doctor came to the inside door and began to sniffle, he wasn't afraid. Nothing much could happen.

As he'd expected, the doctor looked at his feet and legs.

Dr. Chandler said, "Corns or bunions? One or the other. I can see it from here."

Charlie shrugged and tried to get up. He couldn't.

Dr. Chandler said, "Probably those shoes. Good God, look at them heavy things." The doctor's hair was matted over his bald spot, and he had a white frock that jutted out over his paunch and parted with the strain at his belt-line. His rimless glasses were high on the bridge of his nose as though he were trying to see through the bifocal part all the time, and his short, thick arms, bare to the elbow, were covered with black hairs.

Charlie said, "I guess I can't walk any more." He wanted to be babied for a while, like in a hospital where you didn't have to do anything, not even wash yourself or get up to go to the bathroom.

Frowning and pursing his lips, Dr. Chandler came over to his chair and got his arm under Charlie's. "Upsadaisy, easy now."

Charlie came to a stand, and slower than ever before, he crept limping with the doctor into the other room. Everything was pain now, but because it would all soon be taken care of, he could look around and notice things without being disgusted or afraid. He let himself be eased back into a chair like a dentist's and propped his feet on a little platform. On a cabinet near the single window were many rolls of moleskin tape, pink and furred like velvet, and a disorderly heap of knives and scissors lay there or hung from the drawer knobs, glistening.

Charlie said, "It isn't exactly my feet that's wrong."

Dr. Chandler pulled up a white enamel stool and said, "I'll decide. You let me play the doc." He began to untie the safety shoes.

Unlike most offices he remembered, this one didn't smell too much of that ghastly cleanliness which had choked him once. Of course, there were smells, but difficult ones to place, odd, biting odors like creosote on new railroad ties, yet more friendly. He tried to relax, forget to pay attention to things, and he looked out the window at the sunlit buildings on the other side of the street. He felt himself dreading that they might begin to move past like something seen from a train, so he glanced away.

Dr. Chandler tugged firmly at his right shoe and got it off, the sticky sock letting go with a sucking noise. He said, "I shouldn't wonder."

Charlie was embarrassed. Already he could smell his feet above everything else in the room, and he rubbed the stubble on his jaw, trying to think how to apologize.

The doctor said, "Should wash now and then." His small, round chin puckered. He pulled off the other shoe very carefully, as though expecting it to explode.

Charlie didn't feel the pain of having his ankle twisted. Small potatoes. He said, "Most of the time I do."

Putting on a pair of rubber gloves, the doctor peeled off both socks and dropped them into a white cylinder waste-can. He edged Charlie's heels into shallow grooves on the platform and looked at the soles of his feet. "Mostly dirt." He prodded the ball of the right foot with his finger. "Used to have a bunion. Big one."

Because he sounded disappointed, Charlie said, "Haven't been able to do much walking for a lot of months."

The doctor played with his toes and looked between them, then around the sides. "Not even any corns." He looked again, carefully. "No ingrowns. I thought at least you'd have a bursa."

"What's that?" Charlie began to wonder how he could tell him of his legs.

"Infected bruise. Or anyway I thought flat feet. But your arches are up enough, though they's kind of cross-ways." He pushed at each arch with the heels of his hands.

Suddenly, the doctor looked at him sharply, and Charlie felt miserably afraid in a hurry. It came up out of his chest, where all the dust was, and stifled his mind.

Dr. Chandler said, "Say, you ain't come to me with a damned sprained ankle or something like that?"

Charlie shook his head.

"Well, I can't see nothing wrong, unless they's weighed down by dirt." He stared closely, for the first time, at Charlie's face. "You must've been chewing it too. Got a hell of a smudge on your lip. Looks silly." He handed Charlie a damp white cloth.

Not knowing what to do with it, Charlie just held it. Only way was to tell him right out. "I busted both my legs once, and they're acting up again. Can you fix them?" The mustache hadn't worked. He was naked as ever.

The doctor looked disgruntled. "Why'd you come here? Can't nobody let me specialize?" He pattered his fingers against his own knee. "Well, heist your pants back, and we'll give it a look. I suppose you got no money either."

Charlie began to roll his cuffs up. "Sure I do. I'm going to pay you cash." Or he thought he would. He didn't remember exactly how much money he had left, and he had no idea what foot doctors charged. Probably lots.

Leaning close, Dr. Chandler looked at the bare, inflamed shins. "You really busted them, didn't you. Them scars is kind of raw. Shouldn't be walking."

"I got to walk."

"Well, take my advice and lie down for a week or so. Do you good. You wouldn't want to have any of those places open up on you. Cause all kinds of hell."

Charlie said, "I can't help it. Just try fixing them better."

Dr. Chandler tipped his stool back and clasped one knee. "What sort of job you work at that won't give you time off for this?"

Thinking hard, Charlie said, "I'm—I'm hunting one."

"Well, you can't get there like this. Wouldn't be worth a belch except at sitting down."

Charlie looked at the thin lines that fanned from the corners of the man's eyes, saw them deepen, disappear, come back; and he felt sure he could help if he wanted to. "Couldn't you put something on them? Maybe wrap them up so's they'd stay cool?"

"Well, yes. But you oughta go to a bone man. If you do any more knocking on the pavements, you might weaken them where they healed. Shattered, wasn't they?"

"Yes."

Dr. Chandler hesitated. "I'll slap some salve on. Can't do no harm. Then you go find somebody who knows what he's looking at." He fished in one of the cabinet drawers and brought out a brown jar. "You'll think your legs is freezing, but this'll maybe take away the fever from the scars." He pushed Charlie's pants back further and started smearing on the cream.

This would make things different. If he could walk easily and not have to think about what he was standing on, maybe his mind would work better and let him think of ways to get out of all the mess. Be able to walk fast, get more places, not fall down.

The doctor said, "What kind of work you expect to get, looking like that? Why don't you shave? You can't play baseball, can you?"

Charlie shook his head.

"Then why the cap?"

"Keeps the sun out of my eyes."

The doctor finished putting on the salve with a last long smear. "Well, take it off indoors. People'll think you're a bat boy or something. And find some shoes to wear besides these clodhoppers." He glanced up quickly. "No offense, understand. I'm just trying to help you. Some folks need more help than others."

Meekly, Charlie watched the doctor take two big strips of linen out of a drawer and begin to wind them around each leg. He meant well, but a job was out of the question now, even sweeping a poolroom or washing dishes. His money would go away fast as soon as he started getting hungry again, and when it was all gone, he'd still be groping around the outside of things, alone, wanted for Lily's death, no nearer the men who owned the briefcase and no nearer finding an answer to the great big question: what had he done wrong? He remembered, with a sick ache in his throat, wanting to die last night, be killed by a train; and as the salve chilled his skin and made it crawl, as he watched the doctor taping the linen on firmly, he thought again how easy it would be to have things end that way. No getting around it: he'd be caught for murder and electrocuted, because the police and the newspapers had already made up their minds about him. He'd heard such things on the radio, seen them in the movies. Didn't matter if you hadn't killed somebody. Important people were always sure.

Dr. Chandler said, "There. That ought to feel some better. Now get yourself to a good bone doc. Ain't one in this building, but I can give you some addresses. And rent some crutches in a drugstore. Don't cost much."

Charlie nodded. "All right." But he knew he wouldn't. Crutches would make him too noticeable and just give him something else to lug around. And he wouldn't go to another doctor. One chance was enough. His legs would be okay for a while now, and he could start fretting if they got bad again. No sooner. "I'm much obliged to you. How much do I owe?" He pushed forward at the waist to get up.

Dr. Chandler said, "Just sit there a minute. Can't go barefooted, you damn fool." He went into a big storage closet and brought back a pair of clean white cotton socks. "These'll make you feel better."

Charlie put them on. They were too big, and the toes stuck out and lapped over an inch, but he didn't care. "Real nice of you to do this."

"Okay, okay. Here's a couple aspirins to chew. That'll deaden you down."

Charlie took them and chewed while the doctor eased on the safety shoes and laced them.

Dr. Chandler said, "These blamed things keep you from getting your toes crunched and keep your ankles stiff, but they'll pull your knees out of the sockets. Get something light."

Groping in his pocket for the crumpled dollar bills, Charlie stood up. He didn't have any trouble, didn't waver, and he felt at ease and fresh as though he were wearing invisible braces on his legs. "How much?"

"Oh, a couple dollars."

Charlie sorted out two. "You sure that's all?"

"Yes, I'm sure."

Because the doctor sounded provoked, Charlie didn't say more. Didn't want to tell a man his business. "Well, I'll see you."

"Remember what I said, mister. You take care." He waved his finger, then ran his hand uneasily up his hairy arm.

Charlie went to the door leading into the outer waiting room. His legs hurt a little, but no more than he was used to. He could actually go forward on the balls of his feet with each step, instead of being flat-footed.

Dr. Chandler followed him to the doorway. "You still got that smudge on your face."

Charlie nodded. "It's all right."

A huge man wearing a slit pair of carpet slippers was sitting in one of the chairs in the waiting room, and when Charlie started through to the outside door, the man stared hard at him. He stared at the doctor too, then back at Charlie. He started to say something, but just turned white in the face instead.

Putting his hand over the lower part of his face and pretending to cough, Charlie got to the outside door. He didn't want the new, good feeling in his legs to go away.

The man said, "Great scott, isn't that the—"

Dr. Chandler said, "Shut up."

Charlie went down the hall toward the elevator, trying not to panic, not to look back, but when he pushed the elevator button, he couldn't resist turning to see who was going to chase him now.

The man, hanging over his crutches till they nearly bowed, was standing in the doorway of the office, staring up the hall with his mouth open. He said, "Hey, you. Stop there a minute." He came swinging along bumpily, his crutches squeaking on the tile floor.

Leaning out of the doorway, Dr. Chandler shouted, "Come back here, fat ass, and let me fix those feet."

Because the elevator wasn't coming and because the man was glaring so hard from above his puffed cheeks, Charlie didn't wait. He headed for the stairs further down the hall, and he wasn't too frightened. It seemed a little fairer to have somebody after him who couldn't run either—so different from the other times—and he felt superior to the man on crutches who was getting into a league that was too tough for his speed.

Dr. Chandler said, "Oh, hell." His voice rumbled along the hall.

Without hesitation, Charlie went down the stairs, and he hooked his elbow over the bannister and pressed it to his side, using it as a sliding prop. Leaning to the left, he took the steps in a kind of stiff-legged glide. The doctor had known who he was all along, and hadn't been going to do anything about it. There were some people left. Still some who didn't jump right at you.

The record was in his jacket pocket next to the railing, and for a moment he was afraid it might get broken, especially when he came to the first landing where the stairs turned and the bannister had knobs on it; but then he decided not to care. The record had brought him nothing but grief. Maybe if it got cracked, his luck would shift, and those on the other side would start getting the fast shuffles.

He got to the foot of the stairs on the ground floor and listened. He couldn't hear the man's crutches knocking on the metal steps, but one glance at the circular elevator indicator showed him it was moving down to his level. That meant there'd be a shouting ruckus if the man caught him in the lobby. Couldn't let that happen. Yet when he strutted stiffly toward the front door to hide in the open street, he saw a policeman there talking to a newsboy and tapping his night-stick against his own thigh. If he were passing them when the man got a chance to holler, everything was over. One other way. He went through the door to his right where he'd seen the ceiling-high bookshelves.

The room was stuffy and dim, and he stepped right again, away from the view of anyone coming out of the elevator, and went between two eight-foot shelves crammed with books that led far back into darkness. He wanted dark most. As he did so, he glanced to the front of the bookstore and saw three people, two men and a woman, sitting near the grimy window whose backward lettering said, "Old Mac's Shop." He said nothing and hoped they wouldn't either. Maybe they'd think he was going to browse. Well, he would. He went straight as far as he could into the deepening shadows, then edged sideways with his back against the wide butt of one of the shelves. There he closed his eyes and listened again. He was cornered and would have to play for a break. Weren't any lockers here to crawl into, and even as he opened his eyes briefly to see whether there was an empty shelf, he realized he wouldn't look much like books. Better to wait.

The man on crutches gargled something from the lobby, and after a short time, a deeper voice, still from the lobby, answered him. The policeman, probably. Charlie held his breath and listened to the way his heart made the inside of his ears click.

One of the men in the front of the store said, "Sounds like Saturday night at the Dill Pickle Club."

A woman snickered.

Another man said, "Mac, I didn't think things started this early here."

In a high, wheezy voice the man on crutches said, "Anybody come in here just now?"

The man called Mac said, "No, sir, old-timer. Not a soul."

The policeman mumbled something from the lobby.

Then there was a long time when nobody spoke. Charlie relaxed after so much straining at silence and felt the heat begin to clog around him. No air passed through his jacket to help keep it from steaming him, but he didn't want to take it off. Might drop it or knock something over. Sighting carefully through the dimness, he spotted a tall, thin, leather-bound book on a shelf within reach, and he slipped it out slowly, not letting any others overbalance, and fanned himself with it.

The book nicked him on the end of the nose, and though he couldn't see the dust in the air, he knew it was swooping around, making curlicues as he disturbed the stale currents with his sweeping motion. He went blank for a while.

With a voice that made him jump and almost stumble, some-body said, "You can haul yourself out of there now."

It was the man called Mac who spoke, and though the voice was gruff and friendly, better than most, Charlie didn't want to move. Might not be talking to him, and besides, he wanted to wait till he was sure the man on crutches and the policeman were far away, losing themselves.

The voice said, "Storm's over for a while."

Charlie waited, wishing for a back door or a closet. He heard feet scraping the boards.

A woman from the front of the shop said, "Look him up in some of those mildewed encyclopedias. Under P for poor, perse-cuted proletarian."

The footsteps were coming down the aisle beside him, but he didn't try running away from them. No use playing games. They'd see him no matter what he did, and at least they were better than policemen.

The man said, "Aw, come on."

Charlie heard the flashlight click on, saw it shine on the floor, then turn the corner onto his feet. It rose up and glared in his face, blinding him.

The man said, "Hi. Sorry there isn't enough light back here, but the ceiling bulb blew out the other day, and I can't get a lad-der up to fix it." He turned off the flashlight.

Seeing only spots of color where the man should be, Charlie wanted to whimper to him, make up a story about stealing a sandwich or a newspaper. As long as he couldn't tell what the man looked like, it would be easy to invent something good: no clamming up because of a tough face or because the man appeared to recognize him. But he didn't have a chance.

The man said, "Come to the front, friend. No sense choking back here." And turning on the light again, he started to lead the way.

Charlie followed automatically, rehearsing in his mind what he would say. But it was impossible to think that one of them wouldn't know who he was. If he could once get near the door, maybe it wouldn't matter.

The man had already come out into a better lighted area of the narrow shop, and he spoke ahead to the others. "I told you I thought it was him. They didn't call me 'The Bellwether of the Forlorn' for nothing."

He stopped to let Charlie come even with him, and Charlie stopped too.

The woman, who was sitting in a spraddle-legged chair near a table full of old *National Geographic* magazines, swung one plump leg over the other and said, "Don't be cautious. That's probably why you're in trouble."

The man beside Charlie took him by the arm and led him forward. It was too near the front window where people were passing by, and he wanted to break away and maybe go see Dr. Chandler again. Anything but this. No sense in sticking your face in a window for people to look at.

Charlie said, "I have to go." He tugged his arm, but couldn't loosen the man's hold.

The other man, who was half leaning, half sitting on a row of books that lined the front window-ledge, puffed smoke through his nose and stomped out his cigarette on the floor. "You sure that's him, Mac?"

The first man gestured with his free hand from the top of Charlie's head to his feet. "Look. Don't question your betters." He turned to Charlie. "Go sit in the chair at the edge of the screen. Nobody'll see you."

Charlie looked where the man had pointed. A four-section folding screen angled half around a high rolltop desk to the right of the front window, shielding the desk chair from anyone who might look in. For a moment, he was undecided, but when he saw that the door through which he'd come was shut and that the shade was drawn down the narrow middle pane of it, he took the chair, grateful that his mind had been made up for him.

The woman wore a fluffy black dress, and her graying hair, struck from behind by the light from the street, came out from each side of her forehead like a hat with wings on. Her face was wrinkled, though still attractive, and she had too deep a shade of purple on her full, thrust-forward lips. She smiled. "Tell us all about it. I thought this morning was going to be a large flop."

The man with the flashlight, after letting go of Charlie's arm, jammed the light inside his belt despite the lack of room and reached over Charlie's shoulder to take a whisky bottle from one of the pigeonholes of the desk. "I'll do the quizzing, Sarah. Maybe I can use this in my book." His clean, jowly, red face turned brighter as he held the bottle up to the light and uncapped it carefully.

Charlie said, "I was standing in this lunchroom, minding my own business..."

The man with the whisky bottle and the flashlight said, "Come off it, friend. No time for prattle." He cleared his throat and looked around distractedly. "Suppose we better have some introductions. The lady with the hair is Sarah Albertson. The gentleman with the well-concealed diseases is Clay Eggers, and I'm Mac. And unless I'm blind, you're Charles Bell. Which do you prefer: Charles, Chuck, Carl, or Charlie?"

Feeling thin and dirty, Charlie crouched in the desk chair, wondering what to do. Didn't sound as though they meant to turn him in. He said, "Charlie," in the quietest way he could.

Mac walked to a tin tray full of coffee cups and poured a jigger of whisky in each of four. His yellow sportshirt, open at the neck and dusty at the elbows, didn't quite come down to his belt, and a layer of fat peeked through. He swayed back on his heels, smiling. "Now we're getting somewhere."

Charlie said, "I didn't do anything."

Mac frowned and passed the cups to everyone. "I was telling Clay and Sarah that very thing last night, but it remains to be seen."

With the whisky sloshing around in the bottom of his cup, Charlie fought at his mind to make it work. These people couldn't possibly have been expecting him. Must have read about him in the paper and been talking about Lily's murder. But they didn't seem at all surprised to have found him hiding among their bookshelves.

The woman, Sarah, sipped her whisky and lit a long cigarette. "Now let's begin at the beginning."

Mac pulled a high stool over into the light and climbed unsteadily up the two rungs to sit. "Usually means a bad start, but we've got all the time there is. Proceed, Charlie."

The man called Clay had very short blond hair, and his face was round and pale as a moon. The light from the window made colors on the thick edges of his glasses. Sarah had what Charlie had always thought of as tall eyes: large and dark, set high in her head, narrow from corner to corner. She looked at him. Mac, bulky as a statue on the stool, looked at him too, and Charlie noticed for the first time the deep scar that ran from his upper lip to the lobe of his left ear. It made his babyish, once-handsome face less real.

Charlie said, "I don't know what to say."

Clay shifted uncomfortably on the window-ledge and tapped his fingernail against the thick white cup. "He's afraid the cop's still around."

Mac said, "Set your mind at ease. I think he arrested someone else. Anyway, that crutch-propped fat boy has himself in trouble. They left about five minutes ago."

Even though he felt temporarily relieved, Charlie still didn't know what he should say to these odd people. The smell of the whisky bit up at his nose, making him dizzy and confused. Hadn't had anything to eat since the greasy pig's knuckle the night before, and his stomach was crawling. Glancing about, he saw a chipped banjo clock on the far wall and was amazed to see it was only 9:45. He had to pause a minute to remember it was Saturday morning. Things happening too fast, too often. He wanted to go to the bathroom, eat, go to sleep again, hide.

Sarah said, "Please, tell us what happened. We want to be your friends."

Mac grunted, and as he crossed his legs, the stool nearly tipped over. "Don't let that hootch evaporate. It's three years old. Drink it, drink it."

Charlie downed the jigger and didn't feel half as scalded as he'd expected. His stomach rumbled from far away, and his Adam's apple bobbed, but when it was all over, he felt loose and sorry for himself.

Clay smiled, and his white face didn't wrinkle or crease anywhere. "That's better. Now tell us what happened Thursday night or Friday morning or whenever the trouble was. It's not just that we got a bet on it. We think the cops has got things scrambled as usual, but we're not sure which way. Besides, like Sarah says, maybe we can put in a few licks for you."

Mac said, "I closed the shop as a sacrifice. Nobody'll bother us. And we're all friends of the working man. Ask anyone." He paused to take a pull at his cup. "If you get dry, the bottle's there on the table."

Charlie didn't think any more. He started talking. The story was garbled, but he couldn't do anything about it. Things got into the wrong order, making him constantly backtrack to fill in. Felt like a dream to hear himself saying it: Lily, the stocky man, running in the dark, the briefcase, the record and the checks, Nick's Hut, Union Station, Dr. Chandler. He was never sure whether the things he was saying were true. Didn't sound true. And while he talked, listening to their exclamations and to Sarah's raucous cackling, he felt sillier and sillier, until near the end he became certain that he would not only get no help from them, but that he was laying himself open to being mocked and called a liar. He reached the part about the foot doctor's office by sheer mumbling momentum, but trailed off there, unwilling to go on. He hung his head and wondered whether he'd dare have another crack at the whisky. They could dream up the rest of the story for themselves.

Clay, running his hand through his light, damp hair, said, "Sounds like a hell of a risky frame-up."

Mac came down from his stool to get the bottle. He paused to look at Charlie and raised his eyebrows. "You've made a lot of mistakes, friend. Should've kept your nose out of it, or else gone the whole way. I mean, talked to the cops, then stood on your good character."

Clay said, "Bilge."

With her fingers pinching a flabby fold under her chin, Sarah said, "I want to hear the record and see the checks."

Charlie didn't care. How could you avoid getting yourself into a new mess every minute? Things never stayed still long enough to let you get a bead on them, let you figure the rights and wrongs or the odds. He took the record out of his jacket pocket, trying at the same time to think of a better way to tell the story next ime. Must be some way to make himself sound brighter, more in the clear.

He looked at the record before handing it to Mac, half expecting to see it was broken, but it wasn't.

Mac said, "Clay, run down the street and borrow a record-player from Muley Bates. Old-fashioned kind."

Clay got off the window-ledge and stared near-sightedly through the shadows at Charlie. He made a wry face. "Damned errand-boy. What'd you ever do for me, Mac?"

Sarah laughed shrilly. "What do you think you're drinking, Clay?"

Grunting, then smiling wide and easy, Mac said, "Friend Charlie here can't go. You wouldn't expect Sarah to sprain her ankles on Muley's stairs. And I'm the host. I want to talk to brother Bell, anyway. Run along."

The man went, unlocking the side door and slamming it.

Charlie said, "I don't expect you to help me any. I'd better get going."

"Don't be a kill-sport." Mac poured himself another snifter. "Now, what names did you hear talk of while you were bumbling around? Maybe we can use some."

Unwillingly, Charlie thought. "Well, there was one on the record, as far as I heard it. And there's names on the checks. And R. Q., like I said."

Sarah said, "Let's see the checks."

He pulled them, curled and bent, from his pocket and handed them over. Weren't any good to him. Couldn't cash that kind.

Mac puffed out his cheeks to blow his breath at the ceiling. "Now harking back a ways, didn't you have some friends to go to? Can't figure why you hopped it alone, and one of them might have talked sense into you."

Charlie said, "I couldn't think of any."

Sarah was holding the checks at arm's length, squinting, not listening. She yipped and waved them around. "Something in these. I know two of the names. Lily Gonchar was into politics again: at a small guess, the convention next week. Look here."

Mac bent over her, but Charlie didn't look.

She said, "Chalmers Bergnauer. He's been nosing around the lunatic fringe for years. I think he's head of the state delegation this time. Eight thousand seven hundred and fifty bucks."

"Who signed it?"

"I don't know. It's messy." Her voice became lazy and arch. "But this one signed by Bergnauer for twenty-five hundred is made out to Willard T. Atkins: he used to be on the state parole board, and I think he holds a county office now. Looks very obvious."

Mac looked at Charlie, back at the checks, then out the window. "Somebody's drumming themselves the nomination the hard way. Not too bright."

Charlie felt obliged to listen, but he wasn't very interested. He'd already realized that he was mixed up in something big, and it didn't much matter what it was. It was sure to be too far out of his reach, in that other world where people made a lot of money and got a lot of votes. He'd never known anything about politics, partly because he didn't understand and partly because nobody'd ever made him read anything.

Tipping the nearly empty bottle into her cup, Sarah said, "Thank you, Maestro Bell. This looks like a real upside-down shivaree. Might even be some money in it."

Mac stopped, looked at the whisky, and frowned at her. "Nobler thoughts, my dear, nobler thoughts. Let's not hear anything about blackmail in my shop, if you please. The point is Charlie here's got himself in danger. We can't let any shaggy politicians come it over him."

Charlie tried to stand up, but the casters of the desk chair slid him backward, cracking his elbows on the frame of the screen, and he couldn't make it. He said, "I really got to leave. I don't want to get in any more mess."

Sarah said, "But we're going to help you out."

Tapping his own shirt and letting his stomach blossom, Mac said, "Sure. At least stick around and hear the record clear through. You might be able to help us dope it out."

Charlie tried again, and this time he stood up. His legs felt all right. "Don't make any difference. It won't say anything about the ones that chased me. And that's all I got to think about. If I can't find out who they are so's I can tell the police when they catch me, I might as well quit. This other stuff doesn't mean anything."

Mac said, "How you going to find out?"

"I don't know."

"Well, then keep your pants on. Never can tell where these little items you have might lead. Maybe right back to your apartment where somebody clonked Lily."

Sarah said, "Sure. Keep hold of them, and you might wind up postmaster general."

He felt certain they were kidding him now, but when he looked at each of their faces, he couldn't see any hidden grins.

Well, no way of telling. Instinct wanted him to walk out, hide again. People like these and the ones whose names were on the checks baffled him. They were like train engines: he didn't know what they meant, what they were doing, where they were going, or who made them that way. He always wished for people to be simple like a glass of beer, having only one, possibly two purposes. Yet he couldn't take the one step that would put him past the edge of the folding screen and on the fifteen-step journey to the door. His mind sat still, and he looked at the misshapen floorboards that popped up at the joints, each one like a barrel stave.

Mac said, "Sure he'll stick around. Can't go out and get beat up by the cops, can he?"

Charlie gave up. It was easier. Something would happen to let him know the right time for pulling a sneak. He said, "Do you maybe have a place I could clean up in?" His feet were okay now, and his legs; but he felt he hadn't washed his hands and face or gone to the john for weeks. Felt all dried up inside, knotted, and his hands and fingers were crinkled with grime.

Mac smiled at Sarah and gestured back into the dark. "Naturally. Washroom in the rear, right corner. Light's done a bunk there too, but you can use the flashlight. There's a razor on a shelf over the washbowl, Charles, if you care to take a stab at yourself. Don't know whether I'd advise it, though. You got a good start on a beard. Your decision." He pulled the flashlight out of his belt.

Charlie took it, feeling he ought to say something nice. "Well." It didn't come easily. No practice for days and days. "Well, thanks for not turning me in or anything like that. I've had a kind of hard time."

Sarah said, "Of course you have. Now go get yourself cleaned up before Clay comes back."

While Mac pointed the way again, Charlie started through the choked aisles toward the rear of the shop, and even before he got halfway there, he had to turn on the flashlight and sweep the floor with it so he could avoid tripping on books that had spilled from the lower shelves. The three people were being good to him, but he couldn't wrench his mind into following their game. The checks were wastepaper. The record was just babble. And though he didn't feel nearly as sick as he knew he should, he still was in as much of a jam as ever, and there wasn't going to be a way out. Because he felt stronger and a little more alert, he suddenly didn't want to fight or keep running. That would just throw him back on the bottom. When he'd felt slaughtered, he'd had to fight and run to stay sane. No choice. Now he had a choice.

The washroom was only a cubbyhole, tall, its plaster cracked, its toilet seat off one hinge; but when he set the lit flashlight on the shelf over the washbowl and turned on the hot water, everything seemed friendlier. Hanging his jacket on the doorknob, he took off his thousand-mile shirt and scrubbed himself to the waist. He even washed his hair, slopping the water all around. The heat of the water felt good after the stickiness of his own sweat and the dirt. Then, because there were no towels, he dried himself with the cloth lining of his jacket and looked at himself in the mirror.

Gaunt as a cow's behind. Looked over forty now, like he was supposed to. Somehow it made him feel better to begin looking his age. These last days had chased a lot of years into him. He picked up the cheap safety razor from beside the flashlight and lathered his face with the cake of yellow soap he'd been using. Might as well begin to look human, and he could leave a sort of mustache just for luck. Not just dirt, but real hair.

He heard the door at the side of the bookshop slam, but he tried not to pay any attention. He began scraping the dull blade down the side of his cheek, listening to the noise the tough beard made and smelling the harsh odor of the soap on his upper lip.

Somebody called him by his name, so he began wiping his ears. The person called again, and he heard the sound, despite the fact that he pushed the jacket lining further into his ears.

Then Mac came to the door of the washroom. "Come on. We're going to start the record. Clay came back with the goods."

Charlie said, "You go ahead. I heard the first part already."

Mac hesitated, then edged away from the dull glow of the flashlight. "Well, all right. But get your shirt on and give us an ear."

While the light grew feebler and began to turn reddish, Charlie stood in front of the mirror, leaning on the washbowl, and he felt his mind loosening again, coming apart. Nowhere to go at all. Broad daylight outside, and people looking at newspapers. The stocky man would be every place. He closed his eyes and groped around for something to sit on. He'd come all over dizzy, in a moment. Eat hot food. He took a deep breath and tried to bring himself back together, starting in the middle.

Later (he wasn't sure how much later) he wandered through the dark, knocking over only a couple of books, and came to the front of the shop with the dead flashlight in his hand. The three of them were sitting close around a little portable record-player, listening to two voices he'd heard before: the stiff gruffle of an old man, and a young man's nasal. They were all very intent, straining and bent forward, but he didn't see what there was to get so interested in. He set the flashlight down on a table, hooked his jacket over his arm, and thought of going away now while they were busy. Yet even as he thought of walking across the room and unbolting the door, he started toward his chair at the desk and sat in it. Letting himself sag back, feeling shaky, he tried to go to sleep. But their voices woke him before he could fall all the way down.

Clay said, "Holy Toledo."

Sarah tapped her finger very fast on the table. "That old guy was Corrigan. Owns the *Independent*. I heard him on the radio several times."

Nodding, Mac said, "Sure it was. And this is getting clearer and clearer. Well, well. I wonder who old Corrigan's going to boost at the convention?"

Sarah hooted gently. "Doesn't much matter. Their party's a gone goose anyway."

Clay said, "Don't be too sure. Anyway, this thing is dynamite." His eyes were wide behind his glasses, and he passed his left hand nervously over his chin.

Sighing, Mac walked over and stood beside Charlie. "Clay, you're too avaricious. You're not among your shady boy-friends now. Let's get our thumbs out of the empty wallet for a minute and think about this gentleman." He looked at Charlie. "You know what any of this means, friend?"

Charlie shook his head. Mac's high sheaf of brown hair fascinated him, and he watched it toss as the man nodded for emphasis.

"Skulduggery. Sharp practice. Whoever's after you, trying to get these things, is a political blackmailer."

Charlie said, "Oh, I figured that."

Looking disconcerted, Mac turned to Sarah and shrugged. "I've lost my audience."

Sarah said, "You never had one. Look, Charles, while you've been running around town, did you hear anyone mention the name of this Senator?"

"No."

Sarah smiled at Clay, then said, "Well, I'll bet it's Taggart."

Clay said, "Natch."

Afraid to listen to any more, Charlie swiveled his chair around and tried to go to sleep. If the stocky man turned out to be a Senator, then it was all over. Senators couldn't get arrested.

Mac spun Charlie's chair around again. "I've got an idea. With your permission, friend, I'll do it."

"Bet it's the same thing I'm thinking." Sarah clasped her hands and lofted her bosom with her forearms.

Charlie said, "I don't care."

Grinning and looking pleased, Mac said, "I propose to play this record right over the telephone into Corrigan's ear. How's that!"

"I don't care."

Clay jumped up from the long window-ledge and walked over to Mac. He whispered loudly, "What you want to do a dumb thing like that for? That'll wreck it."

Mac paced the width of the shop, swinging his legs loosely. "On the contrary. Maybe Corrigan will get flustered enough to drop a few names. Anyway, it'll dish the plans of whoever owns this record. We might even make Corrigan back out of both deals. Then he'll run himself for President."

Clay took Mac by the lapel. "You sap. What will the record be worth then? Nobody'll want it if they think it's being splashed all over town."

In a high, fluting voice, Sarah said, "I thought we were trying to get Charles Bell out of a jam."

Clay said, "All right, all right. We'll help him out of town. Can't fight a whole organization, and the *Evening News* is howling for his skin. Think the cops will give him a break? Why should we pass up a chance to make some dough, just on a wild stab?"

Charlie said, "I don't care." He didn't. They were talking about things that had no relation to him. He only knew about running away. That is, walking away. That was all he wanted to know.

With one hand on the back of his neck and the other scratching the scar on his cheek, Mac said, "Be a lot healthier and a lot more fun just to play it on the telephone. We'd be monkeying with the wrong boys if we tried to peddle this stuff. Modern politicos hire some tough ones. Look what happened to Lily Gonchar."

Sarah bobbed in her chair. "Then we could call Chalmers Bergnauer and read him a few numbers. Be fun to settle back and watch the newspapers for a couple weeks."

Mac nodded. "The majority has it."

Clay said, "Oh, for God's sake." He gaped at Mac and Sarah for a moment, crinkling his brow all the way up into his thin blond hair. Then he frowned at Charlie and walked back to the window-ledge to slouch there.

Out of place and slightly afraid, Charlie felt the air of the room going stale. "Can I go now?"

Mac took the record from the machine and looked at it closely. "Don't be silly." He put it back on the turntable and eased the needle-arm into place. "Things are just beginning."

Charlie said, "That's what I mean. I'd like to go."

Trying to light a cigarette and wave at Charlie at the same time, Clay said, "Stick around. You don't want to go to jail, do you?" Then, as he saw Mac thumbing through the phonebook, he said, "Don't be crazy, Mac. You can't get Corrigan on the phone. He's probably got about eight secretaries just to keep guys like you out of his hair. And besides—" he glanced at his wristwatch— "it's only ten-fifteen. I bet you won't find him this early."

Mac said, "Watch me."

With his hands halfway in his pockets, Charlie sat in the chair and rested. After his experiences at the record shop and at Nick's Hut, he knew the surest way to rouse the police off their hunkers was to fool around with a record. But he figured he still had a little time to spare, even though Mac was almost ready to make the call. Could still get out and be no further in the hole.

Sarah, one hand on the record-player's switch, laughed and said, "Say when. This is wonderful."

Mac dialed a number on the phone which was mounted on the wall near the rolltop desk. After a moment, he said, using a loud, wheezing voice, "This is Governor Sandblast of Wyoming. I'd like to speak to Mr. Corrigan." He paused and winked at Clay who was looking angry.

Sarah said, "Tell him you want him to hear a speech you're giving tonight."

Mac shushed her and crowed over the phone, "That's right. Governor Sandblast. It's very important, girlie, so switch me to him. Haven't got much time."

Listening hard, Charlie was amazed by the daring of the man. He himself always felt half strangled when he spoke on a telephone. Needed to be sure of people's faces.

Mac said, "That you, Corrigan? How are you, you old blowhard? Never mind, never mind. Just listen a minute. Got something I want you to hear."

Sarah started the record going, and Mac stretched the combination receiver-mouthpiece to the end of its cord in the direction of the player. The voices began.

Glad, for the time being, that he wasn't forced to listen to something new, Charlie shut off his mind and looked around the room. He was just going into a nice daze when he caught Clay's eye. The man was standing up now at the far side of the table that held the record-player, and he motioned with his head for Charlie to come over. The man's actions were stealthy, and Charlie didn't want to go, but Clay's bright eyes and glimmering, white face intimidated him. Giving in easily because he had nothing else to do, he stood up, circled the table where Sarah was chortling at Mac, and followed Clay part way toward the side door.

Barely above the voices of the men on the record, Clay said, "This is going to get you way the hell in dutch. Corrigan will have that call traced faster than you can hop, and then where'll you be?"

Charlie had already thought of that. "I know."

Mac snapped his fingers for them to be quiet, and Sarah turned the record-player up louder.

Clay said, "Them two are screwballs. They'll get you in more trouble than you got, and you won't have a prayer. Now, I got some friends who can maybe wrassle you out of this."

He was speaking so low that Charlie could scarcely hear him over the rasp of the old man's voice on the record. He looked at the tiny blond bristles that speckled Clay's jowls, and he was surprised to see sweat pinpointing the tight skin.

Clay said, "I say I got some friends who can help you. Mac and Sarah won't like it 'cause it might spoil their damn game, but I want to do you some good." He smiled, and the smallest kind of muscle ticked in the left corner of his mouth.

Charlie shook his head. "I don't think I will."

Leaning closer and trying to speak more softly, Clay said, "Won't what? Ain't you concerned about getting your neck out of this? Look at that jerk." He tossed his head in Mac's direction. "Just because the FBI wouldn't put him on their Commie list, he thinks he's got to play ring-around-the-pinky some other way. Fat-headed, washed-up hack. Better duck out with me while you can."

Charlie backed away, wanting to touch his legs to see whether the linen wrappings were still there. "No thanks."

A little more loudly, Clay said, "Don't be dumb."

Mac was bending over double now, holding his ear tight against the receiver part of the cradle phone and trying to keep the other part aimed at the record machine. His backsides shook from chuckling. Then suddenly he hung up.

Charlie was surprised, then pleased that the record hadn't gotten any further than the part he'd already heard. Nothing new, nothing new.

Mac said, "I told you it'd make something happen."

Turning off the record, Sarah searched in her purse for a cigarette. "What?"

"Corrigan exploded, cussed like Sebastian Pratt. Should've heard him. And he dragged over some other guy to listen. Called him Hindruth."

Clay said, "Probably just one of his bodyguards."

Mac picked up the empty whisky bottle and put it down again. "I don't think so. He kept yelling that this Hindruth was trying to swindle him."

Sarah said, "The other guy say anything?"

"Tried to pass it off. Said it didn't matter at all, didn't mean anything." He was pleased with himself and rubbed his sides.

Clay walked the width of the room to face Mac and looked up at him. "Now see what you've done, rubber-brain? That was probably one of the guys that belonged to the record, and we queered his deal. He'd have paid plenty for it, but not now."

"Don't be an ass." Mac turned to Charlie. "Well, there's one name. We'll see what we can do with it, friend. Never can tell."

Sarah said, "Let's not just sit back. What about these photostats?"

Spreading the three pictures of checks out on the table where they could all see, Mac said, "Next on the agenda. By the time we phone some of these guys, we ought to be sitting on all sorts of info."

Clay said, "I didn't see these yet." He went to the table and, blinking his glasses firmly into place, ran his finger over the names and numbers, reciting them half aloud.

Charlie stood near the record-player, forgetting entirely about the front window. They still thought he was anxious about who was after him, anxious over who had killed Lily. That was half an hour ago. They couldn't keep track. Funny he hadn't remembered how big Chicago could get, hadn't even remembered how it went faster than any one person. Made all the difference. He wasn't afraid, but he didn't want to try chasing anyone, getting tough with those who were already tougher than he could imagine. Earlier, he'd almost turned around and decided to chase the stocky man. Silly. Best thing was to get himself gone. Far away, where neither side had to play any more.

Mac said, "Bergnauer. There was something about him in the paper last week." He went to a stack of newspapers between the folding screen and the front window and, kneeling, began to riffle through them.

Sarah was deep in the phonebook, running her finger down a column, her nose close to the page, and when Clay joined her, arguing about a name, he left the pictures of checks on the table.

Charlie picked them up and put them in his pants pocket. It would be a good time to go. He slipped the record off the turntable, put it inside his shirt, and backed toward the door, careful to take steps when none of the three was looking at him. In some way, what they were doing wasn't good. They were having too much fun and were thinking about making money from it. And Clay gave him the kind of feeling he'd had in the Union Station when the stocky man shoved his face too close. Even as he thought it, Clay looked over his shoulder, then relaxed when he saw Charlie standing innocently ten feet from the door and facing him.

When Mac, his arms full of newspapers, strode over to look in the telephone book too, Charlie sidled toward the door, hands down to feel the knob and bolt. Wouldn't make any difference to them. They could think up something else exciting to do, and could keep reading what happened to him in the newspapers. The trouble was that he hadn't known for one minute what to say to any of them, maybe because they didn't work. You could talk about work. But in a flush of embarrassment, he remembered telling them all about himself for the last two days, everything, even the insane parts. Had to get away from that too. He felt the brass knob of the door touch his left palm, and he reached above it with his right to slide back the bolt. It went quickly. Then he turned the knob slowly and with his free hand tugged his cap brim down low, and the last thing he saw was Sarah waving her finger in Clay's face. She was talking hard to him in a squeaky voice, but Charlie didn't listen. He pulled the door open and headed for the lobby's main entrance, hoping the policeman would be walking around the other side of the block, the newsboy eating an early lunch, the man on crutches soaking his bunions, or whatever, in salt water.

CHAPTER EIGHT

A few minutes after ten, Hindruth let himself into the oak-lined anteroom and looked at the secretary who was sorting mail at her desk.

She turned her emaciated, heavily powdered face in his direction, showing no sign of interest. "Yes?"

"Mr. Hindruth to see Mr. Corrigan. I have an appointment."

She glanced in a gilt-edged book and nodded. "Through this door. Mr. Endres will take care of you." She pushed a button under her desk, and the lock on the door buzzed.

Hindruth caught the knob before the buzzing stopped and went through into another room, only slightly larger than the first, and he tried to act powerful. There could be no bumbling. He had to remember everything.

Yet he wanted to forget about the briefcase he was carrying, full of precise personal dirt and detailed records of malfeasance, connivance, and soul-selling on the part of just about everyone in Illinois. He hadn't expected to feel quite so unclean. The man with the whip. He didn't feel like the man with the whip. He felt like the whipping boy.

A man rose from behind another glass-topped desk. "Mr. Hindruth? Mr. Corrigan will see you right away."

Looking at the man's neat brown gabardine suit, at his small-check tie, at his gleaming glasses, his adenoidal face, Hindruth felt uneasy. Would Corrigan be a machine too?

With the air of one performing a ritual, the man swung open a thick, mahogany-stained door, waited for Hindruth to pass, said, "Mr. Hindruth," and closed the door again.

And everything was beginning. In spite of all the messes, impossibilities, uncertainties, and compounded mistakes, everything was supposed to begin happening now. Hindruth took the office like a photograph: good prints on the walls, a Rembrandt of a rumpled old man with a white beard, sitting in a chair; rugs ankle-deep; the old, old, soft-colored wood of the ceiling; the portable bar. And a little man was standing behind the bean-shaped desk with his back against the single huge window. What was the way to start blackmailing somebody?

The little man said, "You've got five minutes."

"Mr. Corrigan?"

"Yes, yes. What do you want?" His voice was cross and quick.

Hindruth moved closer to the desk, trying to compose himself. "Perhaps you know why I'm here."

Corrigan chuckled, then choked on it. "You might as well sit down a minute. If that boneheaded Senator sent you, it's your last chance to be comfortable in here."

Although the mild glare from the sky was in his eyes as he sat in an armchair, Hindruth could see the straggly shock of cinnamon-colored hair on the other man's head and could see, by craning his neck over the high jumble of knickknacks on the desk, Corrigan's food-spotted shirt-front. "I'm only a semi-official representative of Senator Taggart, but I do come on his behalf."

"Which half?" Corrigan left the window and came around the desk to lean against it, his knees nearly touching Hindruth's chair.

"Pardon me?"

"Never mind. It doesn't matter. Well, you're wasting your time."

Hindruth nearly found himself agreeing out loud with the man. No, better to be blunt, say it straight before some irrelevant conversation got started. He settled back, smoothing his fingers over the soft leather of the briefcase. "The Senator wants your paper to back him in the convention next week." He was glad there were no mirrors in the room.

Deliberately, Corrigan spit on the carpet. "I wouldn't dream of it."

Hindruth hurried on. "The Senator has the highest regard for your organizational abilities. He thinks you'd make an excellent Secretary of the Interior. If he becomes President, he'd like to have you accept such a post." He watched the laughter wrack the little man's chest. So this was the energetic, politico-making-and-breaking Corrigan.

Holding his throat and gasping, Corrigan said, "But he isn't going to be President. Not ever. Not even a senator much longer if he doesn't quit mouthing off. How those admirable, voting-age Eastern citizens ever took it into their heads to vote for him in the first place, I'll never know. He must have a flock of relatives."

Hindruth tried to shrug, but the wings of his armchair got in the way. "You underestimate him."

"Impossible."

"You won't reconsider?"

"No."

"It would be a very patriotic move on the part of your paper."

Laughing as he walked around to sit at his desk, Corrigan planted both elbows on his blotter. "It would be outright, irrevocable, fuzzy-headed suicide. That's what it would be. Tell him I said so. And that's the end of this get-together, Mr. Hindruth. You may leave now."

Unwillingly, Hindruth flicked the catch on the briefcase and glanced inside. It had to be, as he'd known it would. While still in the East, he had imagined doing all varieties of buttering-up among those who would fill the Illinois seats at the convention: parties, gifts, whisky-conferences. He'd even steeled himself to the possible necessity of applying a judicious chorus-girl or two in the right quarters. But blackmail seemed a dangerous way to try winning anything as big as the nomination. Dangerous and silly.

Corrigan said, "That was the king's English I just spoke, friend. I said that was all."

Reaching inside the briefcase, Hindruth said, "No, it isn't." There was a great deal to choose from: photographs taken in a hotel bedroom in Mexico City, affidavits from the steward and cabin-boy of a Grace Line ship, and the recording of a sell-out. No, come to think of it, not the recording. He took out some of the photos and handed them across to Corrigan.

The little man inspected them one by one, then gave them back. "Very amusing. So what?"

Hindruth felt his mouth sag a little. He'd expected more of a reaction, perhaps some of the famous vitriol. "I thought these might change your mind."

"About backing the Senator? Don't be stupid. I don't see him in these pictures. Maybe if I'd been in bed with him I'd think about it."

In a daze, Hindruth passed over the affidavits. All along, though he'd not been pleased at the idea of using such devices, he'd at least had the comfort of thinking they were potent enough to do the job.

Corrigan read them all the way through, then passed them over. "Bring back a lot of memories. But I repeat: so what?"

"We could ruin your reputation with these."

"What reputation?"

Hindruth frowned vaguely. "Well, I suppose someone might send them to your friends and your enemies. Give them all weapons against you."

"They have plenty already. Few more won't hurt. In fact, it might keep them happier. Now I think I'm only going to say it one more time, mister. Get out of here."

In desperation, Hindruth thought of Cooper's stolen record. He didn't know the exact contents, but he knew it concerned

Corrigan's sell-out to the other side. If he had it, it might make more of an impression, but only Charles Bell knew where it was. He cleared his throat. "There's something else."

"If my dog signed a paper saying I feed him horse-meat, I'm not interested. Good-by."

"We have in our possession a record of a conversation you had with a Mr. Delson. It would make fine copy for your rival papers."

Corrigan sat upright and locked his fingers together. "Conversation about what?" His eyes were slits under his sandy eyebrows.

"About the purchase of your services."

Corrigan tapped his fingers. "You have no such record."

"I assure you we do." Hindruth's tongue felt thick and uncontrollable, and then there was a calm, during which he kept himself from getting flustered. Maybe it was going to work. He imagined the Senator's pleasure when he saw the turnabout in the *Independent.*

Stirring himself, Corrigan said, "Yes, I can see how it might have been managed. Fairly clever, if true. But it doesn't alter the case any. Now scram out of here."

Hindruth wagged his head in bewilderment.

"What a novice, Hindruth, what a novice. You shouldn't be let out alone. Did you suppose I wouldn't tape our conversation? Anything the Senator can do to me I can do back."

Blushing, Hindruth said, "I don't care."

"Maybe you don't, but he will. Now, go away, for God's sake. I'm tired of looking at you."

Hindruth raised his voice, hoping it would do something. "You're just as involved in this conversation as I am. You wouldn't dare use it against me or anyone else."

"Wrong. You've broken a law. I haven't." Corrigan pushed a buzzer on his desk and waited. "You ought to join the Bloomer Girls and forget about politics, Hindruth. You'll wind up serving time for the Senator some day. A perfect fall guy. It's probably occurred to him already."

The male secretary opened the door. "Yes, sir?"

"Show this peculiar man down to the want-ad department. He can give us some business."

"Yes, sir." He stood expectantly by the door, smiling.

Hindruth said, "If this turns into a shooting match, you've a great deal more money at stake than the Senator. Don't forget that."

Corrigan swiveled his chair till the springs sang. "In a shooting match, I shoot first. Read tomorrow's paper. I'd leave town if I were you."

The telephone rang.

Corrigan picked up the receiver and waved the back of his hand at Hindruth; then he said over the phone, "Yes? Governor who? All right, all right. You can put him on."

Being as dignified as he could, Hindruth went toward the door. He was no better than Cooper. Worse. A ridiculous, graying man who didn't have enough sense to remember what he'd seen so often in the movies.

Corrigan said, "What? Who the hell—?"

What would the Senator say when he heard about this? It was really the end. No way of dodging. In the Senator's book, there was only one kind of damned fool: everybody else.

Corrigan said, "Hey, Hindruth, I forgot to ask you who had the recording, if there is any."

He almost didn't answer. He was too weary, too angry to feel like inventing a lie. But he did. "It's in my safety deposit box downtown. If you want it, you'll need an army."

His face suddenly turning fiery red, Corrigan said, "Oh, yeah? Then come here and listen a minute. I got news for you."

Hindruth walked across the room, afraid, knowing what he was going to hear, and he felt dread creeping up his throat. If Corrigan found out someone else had the record, perhaps he wouldn't hesitate to use his own tape of the day's conversation. And when he put the receiver to his ear and heard the squawky, recorded voice of Corrigan swearing and laughing about the Senator, heard another man agreeing with him, heard them strike a bargain, he put down the phone and felt like a shambles. The real Corrigan was swearing too, talking about a swindle, but there were so many swindles going on that Hindruth wasn't sure at first which one he meant. He made a minor effort to pass it off. He looked at Corrigan who was halfway across the room, jabbering in a low voice to the secretary.

Hindruth said, "I forgot. That's one of my assistants. He was instructed to let you hear the recording at"—he glanced at his watch—"just this time."

Throwing a disgusted look over his shoulder, Corrigan said, "Don't give me any of your goddamn afterthoughts. Get going. I can't use you." He shoved the secretary toward the outer room. "Don't just stand there screwing around. Get it traced. You know what to do."

Hindruth stood on the carpet, feeling everything dissolving around him. When things got this swift, he could only watch and wonder.

Corrigan was at his side. "Where'd you hear about the record? Who told you?" He took Hindruth by both lapels, then let go. "Or did you really have it after all? You mean, somebody swiped it from you?"

Carefully selecting the right question to answer, Hindruth opened his mouth.

Corrigan said, "Somebody hooked it. Okay, get lost. You're one of the most absolute wastes of time I've ever seen." He shoved. "I'm not even going to take that briefcase away from you and burn it. That's what I think of your outfit. Tell the Senator to paper his walls with it."

Finding himself through the first door, Hindruth went to the second, not bothering to listen to the excited babble of the secretary on the telephone, and by the time he got to the tiny hall and the elevator, his hands were shaking, and the sweat was getting into his eyes like tears. A first-class fiasco, and it was all Cooper's fault.

As the elevator sank with him to the ground floor, he remembered with a real nostalgia the days in Washington when he'd only had to worry about keeping the Senator's books fairly straight, keeping rows of numbers semi-logical. You could close a ledger, lock it in a safe, and go home—or go out and enjoy yourself, knowing that the numbers wouldn't do anything to each other while you were gone. Not so with people. They kept doing things all the time.

Charles Bell. He'd even felt sorry for the man, sorry he was being hunted and harried all over the local map by police and thugs for a crime he'd probably had nothing to do with. And now, just by playing a record over the telephone, he'd mixed things up so badly they'd never come unmixed. Yet, of course, he couldn't really be blamed.

The elevator doors opened, and Hindruth went through the lobby into the staggeringly brilliant sunlight and stood on the curb to wait for a taxi. Bell's picture in the newspaper had been worse than he'd expected: a weak, honest face. Easily bullied. He'd probably looked like that himself once. Praksar and Cooper had been chasing the man last night, according to their story, and the night before. But they obviously hadn't caught him yet. God, would it be necessary to tell the Senator about *all* the blunders? And as the cab stopped in front of him and he reached for the door handle, he began wondering whether he could induce the police to chase him too, to put him in jail; for then everything would resolve itself into a simple pattern, and he could sit down, free of others, for a long, long time.

CHAPTER NINE

When Charlie came out of the building onto the sidewalk of Clark Street, he turned and hurried past the front of Old Mac's Shop, not bothering to look in. Didn't matter if the three crazy people could see him. They couldn't stop him. But at the corner of Jackson and Clark, where a traffic whistle went through his head like an ice-pick and the people shoved each other, he remembered to be afraid of everyone again. It was easy to start running away, yet he never really got anywhere. Always still in the thick of things.

The sun was so hot that he didn't put his jacket on, no matter how much safer an upturned collar might have made him. No more baking. Turning the corner to go east on Jackson, he tried to figure what to do. He could keep walking around, but it would be only a matter of minutes, probably, before someone raised a yip at the sight of him. Had to get out of town. How? Well, trains were out. Wouldn't have a chance with them. And buses were full of people. Hitch-hiking was impossible downtown. Because he wasn't paying any attention, he stubbed his toe twice in a row on the edges of a grating, and his legs, though still fairly cool under their wrappings, twanged sharply. He wanted to go far away where nobody had seen his picture in the paper, but he couldn't do it on his legs. Had to have wings or wheels.

He hiccoughed and smelled the whisky backwards as the fumes came out of his nose. Something to eat. He hiccoughed again, bobbed his head up high to try to keep from making noise, and when his eyes, for a moment, were looking straight ahead down the sidewalk, he saw a policeman coming toward him. He wasn't sure it was the same one who'd been outside Dr. Chandler's building, but he was just as big. In no mood to tempt anyone and with no love for the fright that knocked on the inside of his ribs, Charlie ducked sideways into a narrow slit between two buildings and kept going. Wasn't fair to see policemen so often.

The brick-lined passageway, less wide than his shoulders, was littered with old papers and beer cans. He walked straight, letting his shoulders scrape both sides, because to turn edgewise was to ask his legs to get tangled. His blue shirt was getting the worst of it, but it was difficult enough to step over the rubble while looking at it, let alone turned awry. And he didn't want a chance to look back. That always made people come after you.

He hurried to a widened area where the low building to his right ran into another that stretched from Clark Street. The building to his left ended, but there was no alley, no way out. The hind end of what looked like a tavern came from the south to finish the box. He stepped away from the view of anyone looking down the slit from Jackson, and waited. Nothing happened. Just a scared little rail-rat, the kind that jumps up from between the ties when it hears a train coming and gets itself mashed on the rail. You had to have sense to stay put, and he was losing his sense.

Standing there with his back against the chipped bricks of the only short building, he could almost imagine that everything was over. All done. He felt like it. But then his stomach, giving an upward, twisting lunge, reminded him that it was terribly empty. He sniffed the air. He'd been smelling food and hadn't realized it: bacon, some other kind of meat, probably sausages, and—he sniffed again, concentrating—and burned nuts. He puzzled over the last. Maybe bad coffee. The smells led him, in a shuffling trance, further to his left where three smoky windows were opened halfway, facing the area. He turned the brim of his baseball cap out of the way and peeked. A kitchen. Looked like the rear of a lunchroom. He pulled his head down out of sight and began stuffing himself with the odors. They were almost enough.

From the kitchen, a man's loud, breaking voice said, "Nobody empties the grease cans but me." And he began to sing it, changing key in the middle of the line, yodeling, and adding a windy whistle at the end of the third repeat.

In a thinner voice, somebody else said, "Chuck that moldy bacon into the omelette. A little old pencillium never hurt nobody."

The first man said, "Check, Melvin."

Charlie listened to the clinking of pans, the hiss of the grease, and he was lulled by the whirr of the fan, above the only door, that blew hot air out into the areaway. He fumbled in his pockets to count his money: thirty-nine dollars and fifty-nine cents. He could scarcely believe it. Seemed as though he'd been spending money like crazy, but he hadn't. If only there was some way to get food without people looking at you.

From inside the kitchen, the man with the thin voice said, "Prop that door open a ways, will you, Art? Can't get my wind in here."

"Sure."

The small green door, near the other corner of the building, bobbed open a few inches and stuck there. Charlie looked at it, wondering.

The first man said, "Ain't no air outside, though. Except what the fan shoves out." There was a pause and a clatter of forks. "Jesus, you sure these eggs is all right? Smells like I need a gas mask."

"You don't have to eat them. You should worry."

Forced by his stomach, Charlie moved closer to the door. Had to eat. He wouldn't get a chance with fewer than two people around. And he could always just scram if there was trouble. After he'd checked at the window again to make sure nobody else was around, he stuck his head through the narrow crack of the door and waited. The man called Art, who was singing something, flexed his shoulders as he scraped a small grill with a spatula. The other man was cutting potatoes for french-fries in a machine that looked like a vise with a long handle on it. And the door leading to the front was closed.

Charlie said, "How's chances for breakfast? I can pay for it." His voice sounded little. He recognized its wheeziness: scared again.

Art, tall, round-shouldered, and lantern-jawed, twisted his head around and stared at Charlie. "The business-end is up front, Josh." He wiped one hand on his white apron.

The other man juggled a big, wet potato. "Don't kid us. We can't manage no handouts."

Charlie held up a dollar. "No kidding. I pay for what I eat." He was poised, ready to take off if they moved wrong.

Art said, "Go around front. What's the matter with them stools in there?"

Trying not to look as though he were thinking fast, Charlie said, "I don't look too good today. I'd be embarrassed." He smiled uneasily. "Can't you just put something together for me? A sandwich?"

Art started to say something, but the other man said, "What the hell. Squat down on the stoop there, and keep your head out of sight. The old lady'd have a fit." He waved his hand at Art. "Toss on a couple hunks of meat, and we'll split the take."

"Thanks." Charlie edged the door open further and sat down, pulling his knees in, stroking the coolness of his legs.

Art shrugged and began singing as he threw two hamburgers on the grill. "What'll you have on them, Josh?"

"Everything you got." Charlie sniffed. He couldn't ever remember having been this hungry.

The other man, who was shorter, more bent over than Art, said, "You on the skids, pal?"

Charlie shook his head, keeping his face turned three-fourths away. "No. Not yet. I still got some money." And he still did. He'd nearly forgotten about it, except to worry over how little there was. Maybe things weren't so bad.

Art said, "Just be sure to leave the damn women alone. You won't have it long."

Remembering Lily and how she'd tumbled out of the train into the roadbed, Charlie nearly started to tell the man at the grill that he already knew what trouble from women could be, but he stopped himself in time.

The other man said, "Ain't I seen you around here before?"

"No." Charlie wondered what today's newspapers were like. Could they have found a better picture anywhere? He didn't think so.

Art said, "Everybody looks the same."

The other man rested his elbow on the jamb and picked his teeth carefully. He pulled back the lines in his lightly greasy face. "I got some cheap half-pints, if you're in the market."

He remembered that whisky was good for you once in a while, loosened you up, made you braver. Maybe it would be a wise thing to have some, just in case. He said, "Well, I don't know. How much?"

"Eighty cents. Can't go wrong with that."

It wasn't much, and it might help give him a push when he needed one. "Okay, you can give me one of those too." He was embarrassed because he'd never liked buying whisky. People always looked funny at you when you bought it, as if you were pretty far gone. Well, if the two men in the kitchen thought he was a rumdumb, they'd forget him sooner, pay less attention, maybe, while he was there.

After reaching way back into a cupboard and straining himself till his eyes bugged, the thin man brought out a half-pint bottle wrapped in brown paper and handed it to Charlie.

Because he didn't want the man near him any more, Charlie gave him two dollars and said, "That's for the food and this both. I'm much obliged."

The thin man held the dollars and looked at them. He called over his shoulder at Art, "We got a money-bags here and didn't know it." He turned to Charlie, trying to peer around at his face. "Just for that, we'll throw in some fried ham, won't we, Art?"

"You betcha. How about a piece of pie?" He held up a tin pan.

Charlie looked at the thick, calf-slobber meringue and shook his head. "No thanks." And turning away, he tore the paper carefully from the neck of the small bottle and ripped a narrow patch down the front to see the label. Gold Meadow. He'd never heard of it, but it looked all right. With his thumbnail he split the plastic seal around the cap. Smelled strong, smelled like the kerosene lamp hanging in the watchman's shanty. He took the cap off and tasted it: the single swallow was hot in his stomach and cold in his mind. He smiled.

Art flipped the hamburgs over and put the bottom of a bun on each. He was singing again, slowly, off-key. The thin man went to the far side of the kitchen and turned on the motor of a meat-grinder. He took an enamel pan full of cut-up, fatty beef from a refrigerator and set it beside the grinder.

And Charlie, thinking about the food that was going to come soon, lifted the bottle up to take another taste, remembering how it had been to live two mornings ago, and the bottle stayed tilted up for some reason, and he kept swallowing the stuff that came out the top. There were so many fumes to smell. He couldn't keep track of them, and then he thought that maybe it was a good idea: deaden his nose. Kill it forever, and never get whiffs of people and bad things again. If he couldn't smell, maybe he couldn't be afraid. Dimly, he felt his head bump backward against the door-jamb, but he kept his eyes closed, not thinking, till only air ran over his lips, and the corners of his mouth were empty.

Art said, "Holy simoly."

And he'd meant to put the bottle down then, let it rest awhile on the doorsill, and he'd started to unbend his elbow to do it, but his eyes came open a little, saw his empty hand, and he heard the soft crash at the same time. The bottle, inside its paper, lay broken beside his foot. He looked at it, puzzled. Silly thing to do, make a mess.

Art and the thin man were both standing right behind him now, and the thin man said, "I thought you was hungry."

Charlie felt his ribs begin to shake. They were coming apart, and he couldn't do anything about it.

Art said, "He took it in one jump. We'd oughta give it to him for a prize."

A small wind twisted into the areaway and spun up a knot of dust into the glaring sun. The glass on a window, high up the next-door building, was many, many colors. Charlie felt better, and he made himself stop shaking. His stomach stayed put.

The thin man said, "You want another half-pint? I didn't believe the first one."

Charlie let his left shoulder slump and turned to look straight at the two men. "Mind your business. Keep your noses some other place." He didn't like having them crouching behind him, looking, making up odd things to say.

Art walked toward the grill uncertainly. "These burgs is pretty near done. You want them in a sack?"

Using the inside knob of the door, Charlie hauled himself to his feet. No sense staying in one place longer than he had to, and he didn't feel hungry any more. His stomach was full and happy. His nose was dead, and he could hardly feel it when he wiped it on his sleeve. "No. You eat 'em."

He walked into the kitchen and crossed the endless floor to the meat-grinder. It was making a lot of noise. Motors. Why did people need motors anyway?

The thin man said, "Hey, you can't go roaming around in here. Get back outside."

Charlie picked up a piece of the beef, shook it between his fingers, then dropped it into the hopper on top of the grinder. It disappeared slowly and came out a small, megaphone-shaped end like red cords. He smiled. "Is that hamburgers?"

The thin man had him by the seat of the pants. "Don't make trouble now, pal. I'd hate to hit you."

"I just want to see this work."

The thin man said, "For God's sake," and he reached around Charlie to grab an empty enamel pan. He got it under the end of the machine just before the ground meat fell down.

Charlie picked up two more pieces of meat, shook them till they dripped, and he took the pictures of checks out of his pocket with his other hand and wrapped them around the meat, then put the bundle into the hopper, and before it disappeared, he took the record from inside his shirt, broke it in half, and jammed it in too. The machine snorted, whined, and then made clicking noises.

Standing with the pan in his hands, the thin man watched the chunky, paper-colored hamburger worm its way through at him. He said, "You dumb son of a bitch."

Charlie went away. He crossed to the door, held onto the knob, and rested for a moment. Now he was cut away from it all. The stuff from the briefcase could stick in other people's throats and spoil their suppers.

Letting go of the doorknob, he stepped down to the ground, and his legs, all by themselves, took him a few more paces. He should be getting far away. How? Not trains, not buses, not streetcars, not airplanes, no. Maybe he could rent a car. He'd heard of that. But he'd have to give some identification, and he wasn't dressed to be trusted. Steal one? He didn't know how.

Art said, "What's the matter, Josh?"

And he wasn't even sure he knew how to drive a car any more. Been a long time. Hadn't even ridden in one since—well, years. But then he remembered the big, stout lady who couldn't see good, who'd given him a lift on the Outer Drive, the one from Pennsylvania. He could take her car, and she wouldn't mind.

The thin man said, "Aw, leave him go. Ain't you ever seen a man off on a blat?"

Charlie walked to the slit between the buildings and started through, feeling fine and not afraid, and he knew without thinking just what he had to do. Go right up and tell her he wanted to use her car. Simple as that. He'd tell her he was a soldier on leave and wanted to get home to see his wife. She was at the Farraday House, and he'd walk spang up to the desk and ask for her. Everybody'd know her. Couldn't help but remember a woman like her. If he kept walking fast enough, nothing could happen. If you just didn't sit still and wait for things, nothing could go wrong. Of course, it wasn't easy to walk fast in the skinny space between the buildings, because then your shoulders began scraping too hard and your shirt ripped a little bit; but there'd be a sidewalk before long, and the going would be easy. He could keep twitching his face, moving his head, and nobody would get a straight-on, clear look at him. It was fun not being scared. He belched softly and put on his jacket.

A long, blue banner, draped across a restaurant front on the other side of Jackson Street, was doing shenanigans in the hot air that rose from the cracks in the pavement; and five mailmen, their blue-gray uniforms melting together and their leather bags knocking, walked in a bunch beneath it, their heads turning, arms moving as they argued. Charlie saw them and didn't mind. He turned at the mouth of the slit and headed east on Jackson. Another blue banner hung from a tavern, and Charlie remembered talk of a convention. Well, they could have it. It was all right with him, but not important. What was more important was the way things looked: his eyes had never been so sharp. He could see the noises bouncing in the street and, far away east, the Elevated tracks shimmering like television in the heat of eleven o'clock. Hunched till he nearly broke himself in half, an old man filed between the passing ranks of executives and done-up women, playing an accordion with a tin cup hooked over one of the straps. The sweat trickled from under his brown hat. A gray-faced woman stood with her back to a wall, surrounded by crates of yellow flowers, and a sign at her feet said, "50¢ a clump." Charlie smiled at everybody.

Straight to the Farraday House without hesitating: that was the way. If he could just keep hurrying like everyone else, go faster than the stocky man could, walk faster than people talk, he could shut off trouble like a spigot. His stomach churned. Whisky made his legs disappear. He should've thought of whisky before and not done all that wishy-washing around. Should've gone east through Gary that first night, never come to Chicago. Nasty, sticky, hateful place, the railhead where honesty went phut. Best thing was to rush out quick.

He crossed a street ahead of the crowd and against the light, and he nudged his way into the mob of standees on the other side, not thinking about his face, seeing only the rapidly shifting fragments of steaming shirts and blouses, avoiding the patches of bare pink-or-tan skin that threatened to touch his arms. Then he quit doing even that: his eyes were getting too good. He let the shape of the sidewalk steer him, step after step, and he passed a policeman going the same direction and didn't bother to shy away. He was safe as long as he was sure of it.

And he began going so fast he couldn't walk any more. He ran. And then he ran faster, stretching his legs as though he were jumping puddles with every stride, loping as in a dream. And through the blur of people ahead of him, a clear space opened up, a long lane with a crowd on each side, like in a track meet or a game. He ran, smiling. And then he knew the stocky man was up there in front of him, scared, trying to get away, and Charlie was chasing *him*. There wouldn't be any mistakes. He'd catch him and hurt him, throw him down on the sidewalk and let *him* see what it felt like to lose for once.

He let his breath run in his nose and out of his mouth, and he sped along, sure of himself, after the stocky man who was changing shapes and colors on the pavement ahead, trying to be tricky; but it wouldn't do any good. Everyone could be tricky, or tough or cruel, sometimes. The figures beside him in the soaking heat were cheering, or making some kind of noise. He could hear the loud sounds. They were glad he was running after someone, instead of being shifty and dumb. They were on his side. He might even win. All he had to do was reach the figure ahead and tag it. And he ran till he came to a wide, wide street, and he turned the corner, heading left, and stopped. The stocky man was gone.

The air slammed around inside his chest, and he shook his head. What had happened? And then, without looking, he knew where the stocky man was: behind him. He hadn't been up ahead at all. That was silly, expecting too much. And now he was going to chase him again. The old way, the usual way, the way it would always be. Maybe there had been three people: one ahead, one behind, and Charlie in the middle. Always in the middle. And maybe it was like that, everything depending on how fast *he* went. No. What was the matter? He looked around wildly and saw the tall, thin, one-story shops that sold nothing but neckties or socks, feeling the glare of their gaudy signs, and he saw the buildings on the other side of the street, all coming into sudden focus. What was he doing? There was the square, permanent canopy that jutted over the sidewalk and meant the Farraday House and its arcade. He felt like crying, but he couldn't, and he couldn't run. Of course not. Never when they were after him.

And he shut his mind and alternately trudged and floated for a while, and then he aimed himself and crossed State Street in the middle of the block toward the entrance; and though his head kept sagging, kept making his feet swerve at the wrong time, nobody even shouted. He took the curb and went past the glassed-in display cases in the center of the arcade's mouth. There were corridors lined with shops and stores in all directions, and he paused for a moment, leaning against a glass case full of magic tricks and silk streamers, trying to decide which way the lobby was. He crossed his arms and squeezed himself till his lungs worked and he could open his eyes.

To his right was a niche crammed with elevators and milling people, and in one corner of the alcove was a stairway. If he went up, he was bound to run into the hotel part sooner or later. Couldn't miss. He skirted the elevators, moved himself around a lot inside his clothes, and climbed up the stairs, using the rail.

He found himself on a kind of long, angled balcony, heavily carpeted, furnished with slick-topped writing desks and crumpled stationery, and when he went to the rail to look over, he saw the lobby below: bigger, busier, more plush than he'd imagined it would be. It had got away from him, had been downstairs all the time. He glanced at his fingers, and they were shaking. He felt he was going crazy. Had to relax, had to relax and be only himself.

Propping his body against a pillar that came all the way from the lobby floor, he looked at the sofas, the bell-hops dashing around with leather luggage, the wrung-out colors of hats and dresses; and he listened to the babble, the steady rustle of folding and unfolding newspapers. So many people. And so busy. How could he ever find the lady from Pennsylvania here? The main desk looked like the counter of a section-shack on payday, and everybody who wasn't sitting went places so quick. He wished he had another bottle.

A middle-aged man and woman, both dressed in light brown, came down a steep stairway behind him and started walking along the balcony toward a far door. They looked at him. He felt terribly messy and wondered whether they'd report him to the manager, but after a glance, they ignored him and went on. Next time, it might be someone who'd recognize him, and it was all because he was standing still again, forgetting to move. Yet where could he move?

Suddenly his heart started burning as though it were raw and inflated under his breastbone, and he had to swallow three times in a row to keep the pain from coming into his throat. Why was he always being shunted off into a siding where he could think? You had to have something mainline. Well, there was the old lady from Pennsylvania—she was the next place to go—but which way? Up? No, he could imagine how many rooms the hotel would have: hundreds. Couldn't scout them all. The desk? He'd look too out of place, too odd. He fingered the beginnings of his mustache and wished it was long enough not to look just dirty. But if he waited here on the balcony till he saw her fumbling around in the lobby, it might take all day, and by evening he wanted to be miles and miles away, some place quiet and steady.

Nervously, he tapped his knuckles on the dusky marble of the pillar and looked down at the people who scurried around each other. He felt ill and unsure. Either whisky or hamburgers: had to be one or both before long. He edged away from the railing and the pillar, wondering where he'd get enough energy to bust through to the streets again and keep from panicking. If only they had taxicabs driving through the arcade, or helicopters, or the big boxes with handles on them that people could sit in, pull the curtains shut, and be carried all over. He'd seen them in the movies once.

He took another step back, and he bumped into somebody hard. Looking around, he saw a man with a brass box on the end of a stick, glaring at him. The man had on a maroon uniform and a hat with a visor, and his full, wrinkled face was angry.

The man said, "Look where you're going."

Charlie apologized, too startled to run away.

The man flicked a little lever on the end of the stick, and a lid on the brass box, which rested on the bare floor at the edge of the carpet, popped open. With a small neat-looking broom, he brushed a cigarette stub into the box. He said, "Better clear out of here. One of the house cops will make it bad for you." His old face and wide blue eyes weren't angry any more.

Charlie calmed down, feeling silly. Old guys couldn't scare you much; they were too easy to understand. He looked over the man's squat figure and realized he was something like those men in parks that pick up wastepaper with a nail and stick. "I know. I thought maybe they would. That's how come I'm up here."

"Sometimes they come up here too." The man let the lid close with a sharp click and began walking away, hesitating as if he expected something else to happen.

Charlie blurted it out before he had a chance to think. "I got to see an old lady who lives here." It didn't sound very decent, had to be better. "She's my mother."

The man stopped and looked back, no expression on his face. "Ask at the desk."

"I can't. I don't look right to go down there. I'd get kicked out."

The man thought a minute, whisking the gold stripe on the side of his pants with the broom. "Call her on the phone."

Charlie bit his lip and put his hands together to make them stop jumping. "I don't know the number."

The man stood very still, acting patient. "The desk'll give you that."

"But I don't know her name."

"Don't know your own mother's name?" He shifted his feet and opened his eyes wider.

Charlie followed the man when he started to shuffle away. "She uses different names." He felt embarrassed because it wasn't nice to make up stories about people who weren't there to defend themselves. But he had to do something. "Look, she's big and kind of old. Wears glasses 'cause she doesn't see things good. Dresses funny, and—" He tried to picture the way the woman had been when she gave him the ride. "And she talks crazy."

The old man walked faster, swiping his broom at nothing on the floor, getting nervous when Charlie tagged along. The man said, "Don't be hanging around me. My boss might think I brung you in here."

Grabbing the other man gently by the arm, Charlie said, "And she comes from some place in Pennsylvania." He was mad at himself because he couldn't keep from staggering, and the old man must be smelling his breath. "You could find her for me."

The man with the broom backed sideways to the wall below an oil painting and cowered there, looking afraid. "Let me alone. I seen a dozen women like her around. I can't do nothing."

Charlie took a bunch of the dollars out of his pocket and counted five. "I'll give you this if you find her. Go downstairs and ask the guy at the desk. He'll know who I mean. She's probably been in his hair plenty of times, and she just checked in last evening. Five dollars."

The old man looked at the money and looked at Charlie. "I don't want no trouble."

Rubbing his burning stomach with his hands, Charlie tried to get himself stirred up so he could make anybody do anything. Had to be almost tough. "I'll make it ten dollars. You just find out what room she's in and then tell me, that's all."

The old man stepped away from the wall and backed toward the far door at the end of the balcony. His eyes were wide and moist. "All right." He looked over his shoulder, then turned around and whispered. "You follow me after a bit. There's a closet on the right of the arch, first door. But if anything happens, I ain't had a hand in it." He moved slowly along the railing, brushing and clicking his box.

Charlie followed him faster than he should, and they went through the arched doorway nearly at the same time. The old man kept trying to shoo him back, but he followed right behind, and slipped into a storage closet full of mops and buckets. A naked light hung from the low ceiling.

In a brittle, peevish voice, the old man said, "You was supposed to wait a bit. I might've got fired."

Charlie said, "Never mind. Everything's all right. Here's your money." He passed over ten dollar bills.

The old man shoved them into his pocket, past the gold stripe on his pants which was worn to a fringe there. "You stay here, and if I find out, I'll come and tell you. If I don't find out, I ain't coming back."

Charlie nodded. "Okay."

Nudging the door open, the old man backed out and left only his head sticking through the crack. His face was perplexed now, more flustered than afraid. "I'll knock once." He pulled his head out, then edged it cautiously back in, tipping his cap to one side against the frame. "Better switch that light off. Nobody's due to use this here closet, but you can't never tell."

Uncertainly, Charlie nodded again. The man left and the door snapped quietly shut.

No sense in putting out the light. That just dropped you into the dark and reminded you of too many things. Made you sleepy. The mops were racked neatly upside down on a row of hooks at the rear of the closet, and two tall cans of soft soap, nearly hidden under rags and polishing cloths, stood beside each other on the left. A shelf above the mops held a whole line of cleanser cans. If he turned the light out, it wouldn't be quite as safe. Things might shut in on him.

Then, with dismay, he noticed he was beginning to smell things again, the piercing, clean pastes and powders, and gradually pumping itself up from his stomach, the headache came. He wanted to sit down somewhere comfortable, but there were only buckets. No. When you sat down, you got in messes. People took advantage of you. Yet there wasn't any place at all to walk, and he didn't feel like jumping up and down. As his stomach gurgled and wrenched upward at his head, he sat meekly on the floor. With a halo of lint around it, the bulb in the ceiling grew dull and went away.

Somebody tugged at his shoulder.

The old man was there, wavering, made all shadow by the angle of the light, and he recoiled when Charlie looked at him.

"She's in nine fourteen."

"Huh?" Charlie wiggled his shoulders against the wall.

"It's nine fourteen."

It was a whisper, quick and raspy, and when Charlie looked again, the old man had sneaked away.

Painfully, he got his legs under him and stood upright, feeling hot little winds puff out of his jacket to make him sweat. What did 914 mean? Oh, yes. The old woman. Should he still try to see her? He didn't have anything else to do, and it would be nice to have her car. You could sleep in a car. The ninth floor probably meant seven or eight levels above this. A long walk.

He got one hand on the doorknob and flicked off the light switch with the other, then peeked outside. No one in sight. Instinctively and a bit sadly, he turned to the dark rear of the closet and felt for one of the cleanser cans. Had to be sly even when he didn't feel like it.

Once out of the closet, he looked through the archway and down the near side of the balcony. It was deserted. He didn't want to see the lobby again, so he went to his right along the hallway lined with shut doors. At the first turn, he looked down the adjoining corridor and saw two staircases: one quite near him, carpeted, wide; the other at the corridor's end, narrow, steep, made of metal and cement. He went toward the second as slowly as he could. His legs felt heavy.

He paused at a drinking fountain to douse one of the rags and wring it out, and he couldn't resist letting the water splash

THE MAN IN THE MIDDLE

up into his face, bubble around his eyes, and cool him. He drank some; it tasted like whisky and made him shudder. Then, as he walked to the stairway again, he punched open two of the indented holes in the top of the can with his thumbnail.

Because the bannister was easier to reach, he decided to pretend to clean it instead of the steps; so, folding the wet cloth into a square, he sprinkled it with some of the white, gritty powder from the can and headed upward. There were no windows at the small landings, just bare, pale-green walls, and the rasping of the worn-over nails of his safety shoes on the hard stairway made the only noise. After five uneventful turns at the landings and beside solid, numberless doors with red lights over them, he felt sicker than ever and began to wonder whether there was any sense in climbing higher. His legs were bandying with the strain. But he had just enough presence of mind, when he heard the footsteps coming down, to rub his cloth on the metal railing and whistle a little.

He was only four steps from another of the doors when the woman spoke. He looked up and saw her dark red dress, her armload of linen, the small cap perched on the back of her hair. And she was too middle-aged to fool. He scrubbed the railing.

She said, "Who told you to do that?"

With the dry cloth, he wiped a patch that he'd just smeared with the wet one. "Looks nice, doesn't it?" He smiled, humming, not looking at her.

She said, "Nobody's supposed to do anything like that this week. I just dusted them."

Charlie couldn't climb any more steps. The woman was standing with one hand on the doorknob, propping the door six inches open with her foot, and he didn't want to crowd her. He said, "Well, it won't hurt any."

She got through the door, but kept it open with a pile of pillow-cases. "You don't work here. I'll call the housekeeper on you."

Because her voice was frightened, Charlie didn't say anything. Didn't matter. He started up the steps, knowing she would
back out, get away from him, and she did. The door wheezed in
its frame, and he heard her cheeping on the other side, voice fad-
ing, calling somebody's name.

He took the turn and went on up. Still lots of scuffling between
here and the ninth floor, and he had to remember to move. Before
she could find anyone to chase him, he'd be somewhere else. With
a grunt of pain, he threw down the can and the two rags: they
weren't any good. He should have known better. The best way was
to go right at a thing, and not fritter at the edges, making designs.
Had to have tracks, or you sank in the roadbed.

Many landings later, after he'd twisted himself so often in
four directions that his breath dug him in the windpipe every
time he opened his mouth, he was certain, though he didn't stop
to feel, that one of his legs had come unwrapped. Be pretty silly if
he started trailing bandages after him like a mummy in the movies. The ninth floor wouldn't dare be much further, because the
air got too thin to be any good. He felt nothing could be much
higher than all these steps; but when he leaned to one side and
squinted up the stairwell, he saw that they went on and on. So
he opened the next door he came to and looked across the well-
lit hall at the number on one of the rooms: 1003. Should always
think sooner, instead of later. He started down to the floor below.

And he was nearly there, at the only door that mattered,
when he heard the gabble rising up the stairs from far below. All
women's voices. The maid, or whatever she was, was probably
making current events about the skinny man in the baseball cap
who'd been cleaning things for free. They should be grateful. He
went through the door into the hallway, waiting calmly for a man
in an achingly white suit to turn into another corridor; then he
started counting numbers.

Finally, passing the other wider stairway, he had to take the
same turn the man had taken, in order to find the right room,

and he had to trace the last part of the number with his fingers, because his eyes were being funny, trying to be red inside and outside. He knocked three times, his knuckles rapping jaggedly. And the door opened, and she was there, looking huge, bigger-jawed, crazier than before.

She said, "You want some more money, or aren't you that one?"

Charlie nodded, then shook his head. He looked around for some place to lean, but she filled the door-frame. He said, "Can you hold me up?" He knew he'd get enough wind pretty soon to say the right thing, but he didn't have any now. He fell asleep.

With a sound like someone thumping on a tub, the old lady kept saying things. "It's just as easy to be nice in the morning, Kate. And he didn't know no better."

Charlie held his arm over his eyes, wondering whether he was up or down, but light leaked in through all kinds of crevices where the cloth of his jacket was wrinkled, so he took his arm from his face. No use. He couldn't sleep any more.

A different old lady, not the crazy one, said, "I know, but if people come seeing you in the morning, that's supposed to be business. Sleeping isn't business."

Funny how you never knew, when you opened your eyes, whether things were going to be sideways or straight up. He let one eye slit a little. It all came from not remembering whether you'd bothered to lie down. The crazy lady was there, sideways, and that solved one problem. He twiddled his feet. End of a sofa. Yes, he was lying down.

The crazy lady said, "Servicemen is different. They don't pay no mind to what time it is. They stay up all night sometimes."

He remembered wanting her car to get out of town with, and the surprise at meeting a clear thought in his mind made him lunge his body forward at the waist in an effort to sit up. He nearly fell off the sofa.

The different old lady said, "There. He's going to be sick."

Hands took hold of his head and turned him right.

The crazy lady said, "Oh, no. That's just a conniption. I always do that when I wake up."

She was fussing with his collar, trying to push his jacket back over his shoulders like an evening gown, and he swung one hand up to hold himself together. His baseball cap was gone. He snapped all the way awake.

The crazy lady said, "Nothing's wrong. You just dreamed something."

Looking at her again, after all the unreal hours between the ride on the Outer Drive and now, Charlie felt surprised that she wasn't more peculiar. She didn't seem so odd any more. Without the red hat, her hair looked no more messy than most other people's, though it did stick out at you too far, and the square, bumbling hulk of her body was more interesting than funny. When his eyes swam down the interlocked pattern of green vines on her dress, he saw his cap lying on the floor near his feet. He put it back on and felt better.

The other old lady, slouched low in a deep easy chair, caught his attention by lifting a limp hand at him. "What can we do for you, my good man?" She was small and bony, and her high black shoes looked like ankle-braces. Her dark dress was stiff, even where it was tucked under her.

Fighting back the mess in his throat, Charlie said, "You gave me a lift on the Outer Drive, ma'am." He looked at the crazy one. "I—I thought I'd visit you."

The crazy lady smiled, pinched her glasses back to the bridge of her nose, and straightened up. "See, what did I tell you, Kate. I knew there wasn't no mistake. This soldier knows me."

The old lady named Kate said, "He isn't a soldier."

"Why, he is so. What's your name?"

Charlie hiccoughed so loudly that the air from inside him made his eardrums pop and startled both the women. He felt his upper lip begin to flutter for another one.

The crazy lady said, "I'm real pleased to meet you, Mr. Rupp. My name's Ada, and this is my old sister Kate."

He nodded politely and didn't feel very well.

Ada said, "You've been drinking. Would you like something to eat? We've got bologna and sweitzer cheese and the kind of bread you can't slice."

Kate pulled in her small chin and peered down at a watch pinned to her dress. "You'll spoil your luncheon. It's a quarter to twelve."

Suddenly afraid that if he didn't hurry, they might give him something to drink instead of something to eat, Charlie said, "I'd sure appreciate a sandwich. I haven't eaten for a long time."

Ada said, "Good." She picked up a wicker hamper from beside an end-table, sat down on the sofa with Charlie, opened the wooden top, and grinned happily inside. "It's leftovers from my trip, but still all right." She sniffed.

And Charlie sniffed too. It would be so strange to eat. He hoped he'd remember how.

Ada, thrusting her elbows out for leverage, broke a jagged piece of white bread from the loaf in the basket. "This is real nice, a picnic. I don't remember you much, but then I couldn't see you good. I still can't." She tightened up her eyes and leaned his way.

Uneasy, Charlie tried to keep his hands out of sight so the more finicky old lady, Kate, in the far chair couldn't see them. They'd gotten dirty again and felt ragged. His head spun.

Kate said, "Young man, I don't think it's right of you to take advantage of such a short acquaintance. My sister is easy prey."

Letting her big, hard jaw sag a little, Ada laughed and laid a piece of lunch meat on top of a chunk of bread. It hung limply on the bread like a floppy-brimmed hat. "She's got so much money, she's worried at everything. She don't even want me to help a poor, hungry soldier."

Charlie said, "I'm sorry."

Kate dabbed at her small, pointed nose with a lace handker-chief. "He isn't a soldier."

Ada said, "He is. Look at his cap." She topped the slice of bologna with a wedge of swiss cheese and handed the pile to Charlie.

"That doesn't mean anything. Anybody can buy a cap if he wants to."

Charlie looked at the thick half-sandwich and pressed the tough crust with his fingertips. Have trouble getting this chewed down.

Ada shut the lid of the wicker basket and stood up. Her face was smiling, and was red all the way up into her hair. "Let's forget about everything." She rubbed her hands together. "I just want to buy lots of doo-dads. Might as well have a gentleman with us."

Kate said, "He doesn't look right."

"What does he look like, then?"

Tearing at the sandwich with his teeth, Charlie managed to get large, dry shreds of it into his mouth, and he kept chewing at them so he wouldn't have to say anything.

In a croaking stage-whisper, Kate said, "Wrinkled, sweaty."

Charlie swallowed the first lump and then felt really hungry. He gnawed at some more, wondering why he wasn't afraid of the two ladies. Either they weren't like the other people he'd run into during the last days, or he was getting numb.

Ada said, "Mr. Rupp, is your face dirty?"

Wedging a half-chewed mouthful to one side with his tongue, Charlie said, "Mustache."

Ada nodded and laughed. "See? I knew they was some way around."

Kate got up, unsteady on her feet, and walked slowly toward the other room. "Well, I don't know about anybody else, but I'm going to get ready for luncheon. Can't stand hesitation. Mr. Rupp, you're welcome too, I suppose." She set her little mouth so tightly that it disappeared.

Walking vaguely past Charlie, Ada went to the door and put her hand on the knob. "Me too. We'll be ready right quick, Mr. Rupp." She opened the door, then just stood there, not going in. "Closet." She shrugged her shoulders, backed away, and tried the next door. "Sometimes it takes me longer than this."

After she had gone, Charlie ate the sandwich as fast as he could and groped in the basket for more. The first one had merely made him more hungry. He was thinking well now: he could tell by the way something sang gently inside his ears, like tension wires in the rain. The old ladies were going down to lunch, probably in the hotel. He couldn't do that. Risky. Had to talk to Ada by herself, get her to loan him her car, then maybe talk her into taking him to it for camouflage. That was right. She'd have to show him where it was, give him the key.

Then he could put murder, running, and the stocky man back where they belonged: in that other world, inside the train instead of out along the tracks. Though he tried hard to remember, he couldn't quite recall what Lily looked like, not even when he'd first seen her tumble out of the train's doorway, tossing the briefcase up to puff papers like milkweed seeds. Whatever her worries were, they'd grown away from him along with her face. Maybe someone would get sent to prison for killing her, but not him. He felt almost sure now.

When the two old ladies came back into the front room—Kate first, calling impatiently after Ada—Charlie grabbed another piece of swiss cheese and stood up eating it, trying to get as much inside him as possible so he'd be able to walk or maybe run.

Kate, wearing short white gloves, kept fidgeting with them and shooing at Ada to hurry up. "My sakes, you can find more reasons for dawdling around."

Charlie was surprised to see that crazy Ada still had on the same dress with the green vines. She'd gone into the other room to change something, but she looked no different from before. He wiped his mouth on his jacket sleeve and waited.

Tromping to a littered coffee table, flat on her heels, Ada poked among the magazines and china figurines till she found a small purse. She said, "I can't go nowhere before I'm ready. You wait and see who tips that waitress eighteen pennies." She smiled all around and finally spotted Charlie. "Am I too dawdly, Mr. Rupp?"

Charlie shook his head. How was he going to get her alone? Didn't seem to be any way.

Kate opened the door to the outside hall and stood there for the others to go first, and Ada marched out, gouging herself in the hip with the doorknob. Though he didn't want to, though his legs hurt more than they should and he wasn't ready to see people again, Charlie edged out next.

Kate pulled the door shut, then tugged at it some more to make sure. She said, "Now let's be sensible for a while."

Because Ada was barging down the hall toward the first corner, threatening to leave him behind, Charlie trotted after her, knowing that he couldn't keep it up for long without having to limp.

From behind, Kate said, "Well, now both of you wait a minute."

As Ada turned the corner, she said in a loud voice without looking back, "I got to hurry or I'll forget how to go down. They's only one way."

With his mouth full of cheese, Charlie peered around the L of the corridor to make sure no strangers were crouching for him. He was getting flustered again, and he wasn't at all certain that the trouble would be worthwhile. Ada was going strong, would be hard to catch. She might not even listen to him if he did get hold of her, and before long, there were bound to be people like housemaids and things bobbing up to screech at him and point. But he hurried along, watching Ada try to open three doors in a row. She wasn't right in the head.

Kate's voice was smaller, further back. "I declare, if I had a gun, I'd..."

But Charlie didn't listen, because he saw Ada yanking open the door to the steep stairway which he'd climbed just a short while before. She was going down that. Or maybe up. You couldn't tell. He went a little faster, picking up his feet as high as he could.

Ada stopped in the doorway and looked back, straight-arming the door out of the way. She said, "I knew I could find it."

Feeling giddy and nervous, Charlie passed the broad, carpeted stairway and headed toward Ada. He said, "We went right by the elevators. They're just over … "

"The elevator don't come this high. I looked all over for it last night. You got to go this way." She waved at Kate who was coming slowly around the turn in the corridor. "Is she there?"

Charlie looked. "Yes." If he could just think of some way quick to say it before the sister came along. "Can I borrow your car?"

"Why, sure."

She didn't give it any more thought than that. And Charlie watched her, as Kate hobbled nearer, getting ready to lead the way down the stairs. Well, maybe it was better like this. The broad stairway was more dangerous, and you could never tell who would be gawking at you when elevator doors slid open.

Guiding herself by the rail, Ada started heavily down the steps, her heels clapping, her hair up and out, her shoulders bucking and weaving. She was smiling.

Charlie followed, feeling mean because he wasn't helping the old lady, Kate. But then he remembered: if you kept moving fast enough …

At the door above them Kate called down, "Nobody gets any dessert today. You wait."

… then everything would be all right. But moving where? He couldn't go with them to a restaurant. He'd already decided that. Now was the time to get the car and drive till it wouldn't go any more, then walk till he fell down. By then, he might be out of everything.

Lumbering down ten steps ahead of him, Ada said, "Where did you say your wife was, Mr. Rupp?"

And it was no time to be making up things. He said, "I don't know. If I can use your car, where do I find it? How about the keys?" He had to talk louder than he wanted to, and the hard walls echoed the questions down floor below floor and sent them back up the stairwell.

She said, "We'll see."

It wasn't good enough. For a while, he'd been able to control things, keep them going along in approximately the right direction; but now he was riding a runaway at the crummy-end, set to be splintered and telescoped halfway through it because of somebody else's mistakes. He followed Ada down past many landings and past three or four doors that led to the inside world, yet no one popped his head out to yell for the house police, and no one else climbed their part of the stairs.

Two floors behind, Kate's voice whinnied down to him. "I'm going to get angry."

Thankfully, he noticed that Ada had stopped at the next door and was opening it to look through. He limped the last few stairs, his legs flaming more and more, and said, "Well, if you just give me the keys and tell me where the car is, I can get going."

She held the door open for him. "All right." She kept moving into the hallway, fishing in her little purse. Then she handed him three keys on a ring. "One of them works, and I don't know where the car is. I'll have to show you."

Charlie took the keys and put them into his jacket pocket. "Are we going to wait for your sister?"

"I got to find that elevator first. Then we can sit down a bit till she comes."

It was all silly, because the elevators would be right at the first turn in the hallway, the same place they were upstairs. You just went past the stairs with the carpets on them, and there were the big, slick wooden doors with a button to push. He supposed they'd have to go that way after all; it was too far down the stairs to ask a lady to walk, even a crazy one.

He led her straight to the elevator and pushed the button hard, and he wanted to rip the heavy doors open and make the car come faster. They could ditch the older lady here, but she had nearly caught up with them. "You show me where you parked it. Okay?"

"Sure." She hummed and looked around at nothing. "Are we going to eat too?"

Her voice almost gone from exertion, Kate said, "Just a minute."

The elevator door opened, and Charlie helped Ada find her way in. When he saw that the operator was going to wait for the old lady, he thrust a dollar at him. "My—uh, my mother-in-law."

The man grinned and began shutting the double door.

And the last thing Charlie saw was Kate's hopelessly bewildered, wrinkled face gaping at him.

When the car started, Ada rocked up and down, bobbing her knees. She said, "Just like standing on nothing, ain't it."

He leaned his face against her upper arm, and she patted him on the baseball cap. "You feel sick?"

CHAPTER TEN

Robert Quiller watched the two other men in the office and fanned himself with a manila folder. Most of the time it was fun making people uneasy, but he had a feeling that Cooper and Praksar would fidget no matter what he did. As an experiment, he coughed. Cooper jumped. No, it was too simple. And he was looking at his watch, thinking that perhaps twenty minutes of enforced silence was pushing things a little far, when Hindruth opened the outer door and came in.

Quiller said, "Glad to see you." Hindruth looked unhappy. Well, it wasn't surprising.

Hindruth said, "What are you doing here, Quiller?"

"Didn't the Senator tell you?"

Hindruth stood uncertainly in the middle of the room. He said, "Oh."

Cooper said, "We got troubles."

Glancing at Praksar sitting on a radiator near the window and at Cooper in a straight chair beside the desk, Quiller let the gray-haired man stand and get nervous. "I want to have a little talk with you three citizens."

Hindruth said, "What have they been telling you?"

"Nothing. I haven't let them say anything. I like arguments. I wanted to wait till you got here so I could listen to everybody."

Praksar said, "Who argues? We got nothin' to squawk about."

Before Hindruth could put the worn leather briefcase on the floor, Quiller held out his hand. "I'll take that. You won't be needing it any more." He patted it and laid it flat on the desk. "How did things go this morning?"

Hindruth made a vague gesture. "A flop. Bergnauer ran out of town last night or early today, and while I was with Corrigan, someone phoned and played him the record Cooper lost. He threw me out."

Cooper nearly shouted. "I didn't lose it. It was swiped."

Quiller leaned back. "You mean Bergnauer's gone permanently?"

"I don't know. I couldn't get much out of his secretary. She wouldn't even take a bribe."

"Good secretary." Quiller felt himself begin to not pay attention. This wouldn't be the least bit exciting. The life of a troubleshooter for the Senator was fraught with dullness. "And Corrigan was not pleased with finding out that copies of the record had apparently been scattered around town by airplane?"

Hindruth pulled his hands halfway up into his coat-sleeves. He said, "No. I wasn't leading from very much strength, you know."

"I know."

Cooper said, "Hindruth would've fouled up no matter what. Don't go blaming it on me."

Quiller tapped his finger on the desk, and nobody said anything for a moment. "Did any one of you three ever graduate from kindergarten?"

Feet shuffled on the floor.

Quiller said, "Setting all that aside for now, what's this about Lily Gonchar and the railroad man?"

Clearing his throat and speaking loudly, Hindruth said, "I suggest we get out of town before we involve the Senator's name in murder."

"Whose murder?"

"Gonchar's."

Cooper said, "We didn't none of us have anything to do with it. It was that crossing guy. Read the papers, for Chrissakes."

Quiller said, "One more crack out of you, Cooper, and you'll go out the window." He turned to Hindruth. "Spill it."

He listened to the story of the loss of the documents, Lily on the train, Lily off the train, the chasing of Bell.

Hindruth said, "Cooper followed the watchman and the reporter and hit them over the head to get the papers back. He said so. Lily was killed by blows on the head. When Cooper and Praksar went back along the tracks to find the missing things later on, they saw the watchman, chased him, and lost him. Cooper said so. But he found Charles Bell's house."

Quiller turned to Cooper. "How?"

In a high voice, Cooper said, "We asked somebody, like I said."

"Who?"

"Somebody on the street. I don't remember. Some old guy, I think."

Quiller smiled. "Asked him what?"

Cooper pulled the corners of his mouth back. "Asked him where the guy lived, for God's sake. This is silly."

Hindruth said, "See what I mean?"

Quiller nodded. "How did you know the watchman's name, in order to ask about him?"

"It was wrote on his door-buzzer, like I told Hindruth—"

Hindruth said, "That's just one little part of it, and you see how absurd he gets? Think what the police would do. Especially with Lily's newspaper clamoring about her."

Cooper's eyes grew glassy, and he bit his lip. "I remember. I didn't have to know his name, damn it. I just asked where the watchman lived. Everybody must've known him." He smiled. "You can't frame me."

Hunching forward till his outspread elbows covered the width of the desk blotter, Quiller said, "Anything else, Hindruth?"

"No proof. Just that he seemed pretty certain the police would be hunting Charles Bell, even before the news of Gonchar's death was published. I'm not saying he did it. It might have been Praksar, even Bell. But it surely wouldn't take much of a slip to get us all embroiled. That's why I say we should leave town."

Cooper said, "Look, you chicken, just because you're scared—"

Quiller waved his hand. "Shut up. Why did you think the police would be after Bell?"

"I can't remember. Just one of those things."

Well, it was just possible that this could become interesting after all. Turning halfway in his chair, Quiller stared at Praksar. "When did you see the woman last?"

Praksar opened his mouth, closed it, looked at Cooper, and said, "I guess it was behind the restaurant where Cooper slugged her. I didn't pay no attention."

Hindruth said, "That wasn't in the story before."

Cooper stood up. "Don't throw this my way just because Praksar's dumb. He didn't see her after she jumped the train. She and Bell must've woke up and gone somewhere."

Quiller smiled again. "But you both saw Bell after that?"

"Didn't I say so? We chased him and he ducked us."

"Where was the woman all this time? Hiding in the bushes?"

"How should I know?"

Getting up from the desk chair, Quiller strolled to the window near Praksar. He began rapping him gently on the side of the head with his knuckles. "Get any blood on the floor of that hired car?"

Praksar leaned away. "Not a chance. I looked careful."

Cooper groaned. "Holy Christ, you simp."

"Wha'd I say?"

Quiller crossed quickly to Cooper. "All right, let's have it."

"There's nothing to let you have. You could get Praksar mixed up reciting the alphabet. The crossing guy murdered her."

Quiller went behind the desk, opened a drawer, and took out a gun.

Hindruth said, "What's that doing in my office?"

"You don't have an office. If I were you, Hindruth, I'd take my own advice. Leave town this afternoon. Go to Washington. The Senator may let you walk his dogs or something. Anyway, there's nothing for you here."

Backing toward the door, Hindruth said, "What about them?"

"Quite obviously you were right. For the first time since you got in town. And they'll come in useful, both of them."

Cooper looked at the gun. "How we going to be useful?"

With a smile Quiller said, "I'm throwing you to the wolves, boys." The idea was growing rapidly in his mind. It would please the Senator's sense of humor too. "The police will be very grateful to whoever turns you in. Not to mention the sheriff or the district attorney. I can take my pick. Our organization can use some favors. And the *Evening News* will be very pleased."

Cooper leaned over the desk close to the gun. "And they'll be glad to hear who we're working for too, won't they. Don't give me this stuff."

"They'll hear, but I don't think they'll listen. You see, I'll make that part of the deal, and if you want any breaks at all when trial time comes, you'll keep your mouths shut. But this will all be explained to you, I'm sure. I don't care how many times they have to hit you to make you understand."

Although both Cooper and Praksar were talking very loudly, letting their voices get out of control, Quiller kept one eye on Hindruth. It wouldn't help to have him get religion and start a confession series with one of the bad papers. "Something wrong, Hindruth?"

He was near the door, looking tired. "No. They deserve it. I was just wondering about Bell."

"What about him?"

"I mean, what's going to become of him?" He had one hand on the doorknob.

Quiller waved the gun a little, and the other two quieted down. "I'll get this matter settled by evening. He'll be clear. Anyway, why should you worry about him? He's got stuff of ours worth a lot of money. Let him sell that if he wants compensation. What's the difference? The two geniuses here just gave him some free excitement. If he shows up, he can pay them back by identifying them." Bell was a zero. He couldn't really be used now.

Hindruth nodded. "Yes, I suppose so. Just wondered. Well, I'll see you." He left, clicking the door shut softly.

Quiller turned to the others. "Sit down and keep quiet while I think."

He didn't need to think; it was all there. And there was no need to worry about Hindruth. He was out.

He smiled broadly, looking at the whitening faces across the desk. "So you two hooligans came in here and tried to sell me, an honest man, this blackmail material, eh? So you bragged about how you'd knocked off Lily Gonchar, eh? Well, the police will certainly hear about this." He picked up the phone.

Then as Cooper and Praksar began their wails of protest, Quiller didn't listen. It would probably work. If it didn't, all he had to do was switch over from the Senator's side and try somebody else. Couldn't lose. He dialed an assistant police commissioner he owed a favor.

CHAPTER ELEVEN

SATURDAY AFTERNOON

The arcade on the ground floor of the hotel bustled furiously with the kind of people that stared through you with fat, poppy eyes, but Charlie, holding tight to Ada's arm, kept his face turned down and toward her, only glancing up now and then to steer her when she threatened to get sidetracked, and he dodged all the looks he could. She was talking, as usual, about anything that skidded into her head, even though she sometimes only managed to catch hold of its tail. He didn't listen. He tried to concentrate, through the bleary layers of light that surrounded him, on getting away from all this, out of town. He couldn't afford anything else.

When, after many stops, staggers, and wrong turns, they finally came out into the more expansive rush of Wabash Avenue, Ada was talking very happily, and she was holding onto his arm as tightly as he had been to hers. She said, "The garage is right over there somewhere, Mr. Rupp, other side of the street. I remember the balcony."

He looked up at the Elevated tracks, then north and south on the street. There were two parking garages with neon signs and wide-open driveway doors. "You remember the name?" He turned to face her, keeping his back to the people on the sidewalk.

"Well, I have a ticket with holes in it." She felt in her purse and handed him a piece of paper.

It was a streetcar transfer, and he gave it back. "Try again. We got to hurry, or I'll—I'll be late." He was standing in a ruddy fog that shifted and did nip-ups when he tried to see through it. Very bad whisky.

She pulled out a sheaf of cards and tickets. "You better look. I ain't got very good sense about business matters."

He found the parking ticket: Raleigh Garage, the one to the south. And he led her to the curb and said, "I know which one it is. We'll walk over there, and you give the man the ticket. I'll pay." He separated three dollar bills from the crumpled wad in his pocket and pressed them into her hand.

"Oh, Mr. Rupp. I got plenty of money. Don't you trouble yourself." But she kept the bills anyway, smiling and nodding.

The walk under the stout, sweating metal-beam supports of the El was bumpy enough to ruin anybody's legs: the old bricks all weather-tilted, the crannies catching at shoe-soles. And by the time they made the step up from the deep gutter on the other side, Charlie's legs were feeling all unwound and brittle again. He kept them moving. In a little while, he'd be able to squat in a soft car-seat and get around the way rich people did. Just a little while.

The concrete runway into the parking garage had been worn smooth and been streaked with oil by the passing and pausing of many cars, and inside, before the lines of shiny, dimly lighted autos began, was a glassed-in booth with a pay window. Charlie stopped at the edge of the tall, square opening where the cars went through, and pointed. "You go right over there. Pay the man at the window." He put the ticket in her hand.

"Where?" She looked around vaguely.

He aimed her by the shoulders and gave her a steady push. As he watched her go, he noticed the lanky colored man who was lounging further inside and smoking a cigarette. He would probably be the one to bring out the car. And it might come down the spindly-looking ramp from the second floor. Wouldn't be long now. Ada fussed at the window, passing over money and tickets, including the streetcar transfer. Charlie waited, facing the dim inside of the building, not the least bit tempted to watch the traffic or the people that squeaked their shoes on the pavement behind him. Maybe in just a few seconds.

The ticket was stamped and handed to the colored man, and he walked off toward the back, not going up the ramp. Charlie shuffled his feet and signaled to Ada to come over and stand with him, but she was chittering through the round hole in the pay window. He felt fleeced without her, lost.

Suddenly he remembered that he had the car keys in his pocket. He pulled them out and stared at them. This would raise all kinds of fuss, and one of the men, either the colored man or the pay-window man, would be talking to him, angry with him, maybe even recognizing him. For a moment, he considered ducking out into the street or running over to give the keys to Ada; but those choices were no good. People still involved. While he stood trembling, hating himself for forgetting easy things, the dusty blue Plymouth with Pennsylvania license plates coughed and chugged out of its place near the end of the line and headed for the front entrance. His head hurt. Ada made such funny things happen.

The car stopped with its bumper just barely edged into daylight at the entrance, and as the colored man climbed out of the door by the driver's seat, Charlie came in the other side, trying hard to remember how to make a car go. There was a thing called the clutch that you had to keep tromping on now and then, a gas pedal, and the gearshift. He began sliding over in front of the wheel, but Ada crawled in through the other door and beat him to it. She plopped down, pulled the seat forward till her knees angled up high, slammed the door, and peered at Charlie.

She said, "Where'll we go first?"

He didn't want her along. How had she got that idea in her head? It was bad enough having to depend so entirely on screwballs, but when they started taking over and making you change all your ideas, you were bound to wind up being a screwball yourself, and that meant a lot of grief. Now it would take a crowbar to get her out of the car. "I thought you gave me the keys."

"Oh, I've got all kinds." She rattled her purse at him.

He had to make the best of it, though he didn't feel up to a long ride with her. She probably couldn't even see the road. "Turn left here, go south on Wabash for a ways, then cut over left to Michigan when things thin out."

She let out the emergency brake and honked the horn. "I won't remember all that. I got to work one thing at a time." She shifted gears.

It wasn't too easy to be alert and help her drive: the windows were mottled with reddish dust, and she never did what was expected anyway. Luckily, the car sputtered out onto the street when there was a gap in traffic, narrowly missing one of the El supports, and she steered it rather well past the rows of parked cabs to the first corner. There she stopped for the light.

Charlie said, "How can you tell when to stop?"

"I see colors pretty good. Can't tell what shape some things has, but I see red and green okay." She patted his knee. "Don't you fret, Mr. Rupp."

But he did. The next three blocks were hair-raising. There was always just enough room for the other cars to get out of her way, but once she nicked fenders with an empty police car. She had a way of living that he couldn't learn: she didn't know, didn't care, just went. His nerves weren't good enough, eyes too good. The heat of the motor swept back at him. He didn't like it.

She said, "How long you on furlough? You ain't never told me."

He dodged that, feeling guilty. "Turn left here for a block. Then you go right on Michigan."

She turned on the windshield wipers, and they skidded over the gritty dust on the glass, making no impression. "I can't figure whether my specs is dirty or what. Things is fuzzier than they should be."

But they made the turn without hitting anything and crawled and stopped, crawled and stopped, till they could suddenly careen right, against a policeman's outstretched arm-signal, and take an unsteady course south on Michigan Avenue, occupying a lane and a half. Charlie breathed again. Well, she was probably no worse a driver than he would have been; no one could notice him with her around, and taking the car by himself would have amounted to swiping it. He'd never have brought it back. "You go straight for a while."

She nodded. "I'm good at that if it ain't too straight. Are we going to eat somewhere? Or is there a party? I don't mean to be a baby, but I can't drink so much. My husband never left more than a smidgen in any bottle, and I never learnt good." She took her eyes off the road to aim her hard, heavy chin at Charlie. "That was when he was alive, of course."

He tipped back his baseball cap and wiped the sweat from below his widow's peak, feeling that his hair had grown greasy since he'd put a cap on. He was getting sleepy in spite of the tension that made him unable to bend his head forward. Always sleepy. His brains were like stale bread.

She said, "I don't know where I'm going."

It woke him from a stupor, and he looked out the side window in time to see the eerie brownstone of the Armory drifting by. "Turn left here."

She wheeled into the turn just as the yellow was changing to red and crowded a car, which had been about to pass, to the wrong side of the street; after a short block, Charlie helped her spin the steering wheel so they could go south on Indiana. He didn't know where they were headed either, or why he picked this way. Probably should have gone north, got lost somewhere in Wisconsin; but he'd never known much about Evanston and those other funny places on the way, like Winnetka, and he had a feeling that policemen would be less thick and more easy to him in places where there wasn't much money. The South Side, then maybe down toward Burnham.

The car was rattling more than he'd remembered from his other ride: the fenders shook, the pane of glass beside him clattered in its frame, and the sun visor above the windshield flapped around like a fan and threatened to fall off. They went up over the short, curving viaduct past Donnelley's, then zoomed down into South Parkway, where the sparse, flea-bitten grass at curbside and in the center lane gave out a green like the unhealed scars on his shins once had. It was getting even hotter in the car, but he didn't want to take his jacket off. Judging by the baked stupor that shone on the faces of the colored people who lounged around the parkway or stood in clusters, it was worse outside. He felt woozy, and his mouth tasted like swiss cheese.

Ada said, "Is this where the colored people live?" She was trying to peer through the windshield at the people in the long, dented taxicabs.

"Yes." He felt safe in this neighborhood. If what he'd read in the papers was right, the police had more to do around here on Saturday than hunt for an out-of-state white man.

Ada said, "It's wonderful. I never seen so many." She clicked bumpers with a jammed-full eight-passenger Dodge.

It was like driving between two high cliffs: the unbroken lines of houses on either side were dark and raw, yet protective. Candy and ice cream wrappers, pop and beer bottles, and shredded newspapers lay strewn over everything as though they floated and belonged like birds. Charlie unbuttoned his jacket: he knew he wasn't imagining the smell of frying, but he didn't know whether it was himself or food from outside. The whole place was a valley made of food, choked with it, and he was hungry. He said, "Maybe we can eat along here somewhere." Funny, he didn't feel so much in a hurry any more. He realized he should be wanting to speed along at sixty miles an hour, aiming down the state line till he was beyond Cook County on this side and Lake County on the other. But he felt lazy. Nobody had chased him, really, since early in the morning; it was the longest spell he'd had since Thursday night, outside of sleeping. Maybe his picture hadn't been in the Saturday papers. Maybe people had forgotten his face since then, forgotten Lily's face too, just as he had.

Ada said, "Why, sure. You point at the place when it goes by."

And it was too much of a strain, when he was feeling lazy, to have to help Ada compete in this big-league driving against men and boys who made near-misses their daily bread. If there'd be a small place off the main drag where they could eat something solid and maybe have a beer, then he knew his thoughts, now so limp and piecemeal, might get together and tell him what to do next.

Outside of the divided north and south lanes of South Parkway, there were two more streets that went along directly in front of the houses and stores. These, he saw, were crammed with parked cars and were too busy. At the next stoplight, he had Ada turn and cross the outside-right street into the backwaters. He wound down his window, saw a restaurant of sorts, signaled her to a parking place, and waited meekly for her to back in, bump forwards and backwards against the other cars five times, pull savagely at the wheel, sweating happily and talking, till the tires were less than a foot from the curb. Then he got out and held the door while she bucked, edged her way over, clutched her skirt down, and stood up beside him.

She said, "These people good friends of yours, Mr. Rupp? I don't look too dressed-up for Saturday, I'm afraid." She poked ineffectively at her loose, graying hair and adjusted her glasses higher on her nose. "I didn't wear no hat. I'll probably get a sun-stroke."

Charlie looked at the place: a long, one-story shop from which cream-colored paint hung in curling strips. The sign over the smudged glass of the door's upper half said, "Lola's Lunch," and more signs, scrawled in whitewash on the outside of the windows, mentioned beer and fried fish. It was enough. It looked quiet and safe, and squinting through the loop of a whitewash B, he saw that customers were scarce. He towed Ada inside, led her over the bare board floor to a booth, and sat opposite her, facing front, feasting with his nose on what simply had to be fish and french-fries.

Ada said, "This is real nice."

A paunchy Negro, sitting at the counter near the coffee urn, turned halfway on his stool to stare at them suspiciously, and his smooth, bulbous cheek flattened his shirt collar on that side.

Charlie didn't squirm. He remembered the way new section-hands had looked at him long ago.

Booths, counter, two doors at the back, one window, and only the light from outside made smoky by the inside air. The low, fly-specked ceiling, and between Ada and him, the wooden table-top covered with greasy plates, fishbones, and empty glasses.

From the bottom of his weariness he said, "Is it okay if we stay here awhile?"

Ada leaned toward him. "Why, sure. Smells real good." She patted his hand, and when he took it away, patted her own. "Don't you feel right?"

A colored woman, wearing a clean white apron, came to their booth and began clearing away the dishes and bones. She didn't smile or say anything right away, and Charlie noticed her soft, tan complexion and her lipstick the deep color of ragweed buds.

Ada chatted away, asking the young woman questions which she didn't answer, and during the brief, snappy pauses, Charlie managed to get in an order for two batches of fish and fries, for a beer and a cup of tea.

Ada said, "I'll try that beer if you want me to." She blushed and made the wrinkles in her mouth show up. "I got to learn sometime."

He said, "No." No use lighting another fuse.

After the table-top had been wiped off and the woman had gone through the right-hand door at the back, Charlie sat trying to give the shortest answers he could think of to Ada's questions and exclamations. She was too silly, and he wasn't in the mood to be bright and silly with her. People whose eyes weren't sharp took a long time to find out simple things.

Ada said, "Does only colored folks live around here?" Pause. "What happens when it gets night-time?" Pause. "Where's all the kids at?" Pause. "What kind of fish will they be?" Pause. "Once I caught a fishbone between my tongue and that thing that hangs down wobbly at the back of your throat, you know." Pause. "Is they any Indians in Chicago? Kate didn't hardly tell me a thing last night." Pause. "Where's a colored church?" Pause. "I used to wish I was colored or a Indian."

He knew he was putting in answers and comments from time to time, but after he'd said them, he couldn't remember what they were. All he noticed was that the things she said were getting further and further apart. And when the food came and he began pulling the bones out of the fish like little, dead fern leaves, she had less and less to say. The beer was cold and sleepy, and he parceled it out into small gulps along with what he ate. You could grunt answers better with your mouth full.

He could tell when he was done eating by how sleepy he was, how full, how alone. He pulled his feet up onto the high-backed wooden bench and leaned against the wall, letting his baseball cap tip forward over his eyes. He tilted his body sideways away from the table and curled it to pretend he was lying down. And he didn't try any more answers. Not now. He clasped his hands over his shins to soothe them for running later. And the last thing he remembered was Ada's rocking him back and forth by the shoulder and saying, "There, there, there, there, there ... "

Somebody standing nearby blew his nose like air spluttering out of a ripped inner tube, and Charlie woke so fast that his elbows shot away from his sides: one cracking the back of the booth and the other making a plate slide to the far corner of the table. After the first panic, he steadied himself and looked around. Ada was gone, and when he craned his neck to see through the front window, it was getting so dusky outside he could scarcely find the Plymouth. But it was there. He fumbled automatically for the watch in his vest pocket. No pocket, no vest, no watch. He'd forgotten that. And as he glanced around the inside of the restaurant, he could find no clock. Never could get things located right in time any more, never could feel that things were clicking and turning at the right speed.

He got his feet to the floor under the table and was sure of one thing: he'd been asleep for a long time. His sore back, the off-beat throbbing of his knees. Yet he felt stronger than before, much stronger, and most of the whisky had gone away, leaving only a kind of darkness in his mouth and throat.

Had to go to the bathroom, then find Ada and get moving again. A row of shaded lights had been turned on over the counter, and as he stood up to hunt for the john in the rear, he saw by their light all the colored people watching him. Men and women huddled in other booths: young men in loud shirts chattered at the counter or stood holding beer bottles; a scrawny old man was tipping a paper sack of coffee into the top of the urn. But most of them looked his way while he tried to walk straight. None of the faces hated him—he saw that at a glance—but they all watched with a kind of quiet, dead interest that embarrassed him, made him feel filthy and guilty.

At the back of the long room he found no signs or anything, just the two doors ten feet apart. One of them was a swinging door, so he tried that first, nudging it till he could see through the crack. It was a kitchen, and he was taking his hand away from the door to try the other one when somebody shoved it from inside, knocked it against his knuckles, and nearly spilled a tray of dishes over him.

It was a young colored girl, hair done up in a tall knot, wearing a red print apron. She said, "What you looking for?"

"Bathroom." He smiled, not wanting to frighten her.

"Inside past the stove." She circled him, balancing the tray, and went toward the front.

Feeling awkward, he entered the kitchen and apologized with a humble nod to a white-haired old lady who was stirring a huge pot of chili; but because she was twisting her lips into all kinds of shapes and didn't pay any attention to him, he went past the massive, hot range and found the john.

When he came out, after having doused himself with cold water till the short, tiny bristles of his new mustache stood out too straight to be dirt, he felt he ought to say something to the old lady. "Good evening."

She leaned over the pot of chili and stared into it as though the sound had come from there.

He smiled, pretending she'd been nice to him, but as he did, he saw over her shoulder a foot-square hole in the wall, based with a shelf, that led into another room; and out of that hole the sound of Ada's laugh rolled like the odor of old gravy, deep and familiar. He left through the swinging door and stood looking at the only other door in the back wall. She was in there, in a room or something. Why was she always hooking herself into nutty places? He wanted to go now, take her with him, but he didn't know exactly why. He had keys in his pocket that would probably fit the car, and he might even be able to drive it himself for a ways; yet he couldn't steal it and leave her in a spot like this. Sooner or later, the colored people might misunderstand her or somehow get her into trouble.

He went to the other door. He wanted to peek through the keyhole and see what kind of a mess she was in, but he knew, without looking back, that nearly all the people in the front of the restaurant had their eyes on him. Like being in a scary show. He knocked on the door then, remembering that you could always more or less run.

The colored lady who came to the door was broad and graceful. She stood poised on little high-heeled shoes, her purple dress
rustling against the jamb, looking at him. "Yes?"

He saw the ease in her large hands, and he didn't feel afraid for
Ada any more. "Er—is my lady friend here? Could I talk to her?"

"You mean Miss Ada?" She looked back over her shoulder
anxiously.

A little child started to bawl from inside the room, its voice
whooping up to a high note, then breaking. The woman left
Charlie standing in the doorway, and with her out of the way, he
could see Ada walking around, dragging a hip-high colored boy
after her. Charlie took a half step to get a full view of everything.
The woman who'd answered the door was trying to pat the boy
on the head, but Ada was making pretty good speed with him,
and it wasn't easy to do. What was going on? The room, thickly
furnished with dark-upholstered sofas and chairs, a television set,
and spindly tables, was not too large, yet evidently led back into
more rooms; the walls were painted brown, and all the lights and
lamps aimed straight up, making the ceiling the most important
part. It smelled like children. There were three of them, counting
the one Ada was leading, two girls and a boy, dressed brightly
and out of kilter with the sober colors of the room.

Ada said, "It's mahogany. Anybody'd tell you." She tapped
her fist on an end-table.

A young white man, wearing a light-weight green suit and a
rainbow necktie, stood with his back to a highly polished upright
piano and, using a large leather notebook as a writing pad, was
filling out a yellow form with a pencil. His stringy, straw-colored
hair was only half combed, and his spotty complexion made him
look nervous and fidgety in the indirect light. At one end of the
long sofa, a thin middle-aged colored woman sat.

The younger woman in the purple dress said, "You hush now,
Roy." She got hold of the little boy long enough to tuck his shirt-
tail into his shorts.

And Ada, walking with the boy to the piano, elbowed the white man gently in the ribs, then thumped the piano till the strings sang. "Mahogany too. You put that down there on the paper where it belongs, you hear?"

When Ada's glasses flashed his way, Charlie tried to signal her, but he knew it wouldn't work. Not a speck of sense in meeting a new batch of strangers. Especially the white man who might be a policeman or something. He looked sort of official, jotting down notes on the yellow form.

The young man edged away from the piano and Ada. He chewed the end of his pencil and walked over to feel the smooth sofa material.

One of the little girls, about twelve or thirteen, got out of the young man's way when he made more notes by the sofa, and she looked at his fingers suspiciously after he'd pawed the fabric. She looked like she was going to sneeze, but Charlie hoped she wouldn't. He wanted all this, whatever it was, to finish up quickly.

The woman who'd let him in the door said, "Miss Ada, there's a gentleman to see you."

Ada turned around and squinted at the door, patting the little boy on the shoulder as he tried to duck away from her, beginning to cry again. She said, "That you, Mr. Rupp? Did you rest all right?"

Charlie stepped backward into the restaurant part, frightened. Ada said, "I can't see him."

The young woman, her hands fluttering uneasily at the pleats of her skirt, came toward him. "Won't you come in?"

He could tell by the way she said it that she didn't want him to, and he agreed with her; but before he could make up his mind what to do, Ada had groped her way awkwardly through the door, bringing the boy along, and had taken him by the arm.

Ada said, "You can help. This is real interesting."

Speaking low and fast, he said, "Let's get going. We'll be late for the party, and it'll be over, maybe."

Ada brought him back into the room and let the little boy go for a while. "This won't take but a minute or two. I never met such nice people, and we can help them get more money." She pointed at the young white man who was hunching himself behind the television set and writing on the yellow paper. "That man isn't going to loan them enough money on their furniture and things. I can tell. I got better eyes than him."

The large, graceful colored woman said, "This here's embarrassing. It don't seem right to have company at a time like this."

Charlie said, "We got to be going anyway."

Turning the little bicep-length sleeves of her dress back one turn, Ada linked her arm more firmly with Charlie's and shuffled him over to the piano. "While you was asleep, I been meeting these folks for a chat. They're going to build another room along outside of this in the weeds, and they got to get loaned—" She broke off and went over to poke the loan-man in the arm. "How much you going to write down that TV for?"

The man's voice was thin. "I told you I don't write down any money for these things. I just make a list. See?" He held up the yellow paper.

"I bet you got a code or some such. You act your age, mister." Ada shook the baggy belt-line of her dress and put her arm around the large colored woman.

Charlie looked over his shoulder at the wall where the small window led to the kitchen. He could see the old woman's face there, and in spite of the steam rising up in front of her, he thought he saw her stick out her tongue.

The very thin colored lady on the sofa said, "Pardon me."

And Charlie looked at her, but nothing was happening. Because his legs were hurting a little, he leaned against the piano and tried to be small.

The large colored woman said, "Don't put yourself out none, Miss Ada. I appreciate you helping and all, but we'll be okay."

Ada detached herself and headed for the loan-man again. She made patting gestures at everybody. "We got to be very careful about this." She followed the man to the doorway of the next room. "Mr. Rupp's a soldier, and he knows lots about what things cost."

Charlie felt the dwindling wad of money in his pocket. Maybe if he gave these people twenty dollars, Ada would halfway forget about them and agree to leave. But it wouldn't be long before he'd need all he could get himself.

The loan-man said, "For the last time, lady, will you quit hanging on me? I'm not cheating anybody. It isn't me that gives out the dough."

Ada said, "Well, that's Mr. Rupp over there somewhere, and he's going to keep watching you too. Ain't you, Mr. Rupp?"

Charlie looked sheepishly at the two colored women. He didn't know very much about furniture, but this stuff was apparently pretty good. Maybe the best thing to do would be to go back into the restaurant and wait till Ada got tired of all this.

The large colored woman said, "We just don't want any trouble." And she looked at Charlie for a long time.

Ada said, "He's going into the other room. We better go too." Then she said in a loud whisper, "Never trust nobody around your icebox."

Very sweetly, the thin colored woman on the sofa said, "Pardon me, I'm sure."

Charlie glanced at her quickly, but not in time. Did she have the hiccoughs?

Coming across the living room like an unhitched barge, Ada reached for Charlie to take him along, but he stepped backward, hoping one of the other ladies would decide the game was over. He smelled the hard, hot odor of the kitchen as it swept through the little window and up the wall, and it felt like boiler-steam on the back of his neck. Well, somebody was going to pull all the pins out of this train in a minute. He could feel it coming.

Ada took a handful of his shirt. "We got to be good people, and you know what the men is like in Chicago."

The large colored woman walked toward them, looking helpless and confused. "You been real nice, Miss Ada. Maybe you better sit down awhile."

Through the foot-square window, the old, white-haired woman said, "You going to hock the floor out from under us. You forget folks easy, you."

The large colored woman said, "Hush, Grandma."

Ada was tugging at him, but Charlie turned again to look at the old woman, who, using the chili-pot dipper like an old-fashioned sling-shot, suddenly let fly a batch of smoking chili through the window and all over the back of his jacket. He tripped out of the way when the next dipperful came arching through, and it splattered on Ada's bosom and rolled down the green vines on her dress.

Hurrying to one of the easy-chairs, the large colored woman took the cushion from it and barricaded the window to the kitchen. She said, "I'm real sorry."

Charlie was afraid to shake himself for fear of getting more chili on the rug, so he waited, watching Ada scoop at the splotches on her dress. Not long before, he would have been grateful for having food thrown at him, but now he was still full of fish and potatoes.

Ada said, "My, it's hot." She shifted the palmful of chili she'd collected from hand to hand, and laughed in a rumbling voice. "I don't think I want any, right this minute."

All three of the children were laughing too, in spite of the shushing of the large colored woman who still held the cushion over the small window. The oldest girl, her long legs unsteady from laughing, buckled over at the waist and chirped shrilly.

Though he didn't mind too much being poked fun at, Charlie was uneasy at the way everything had stopped momentarily. Ada, hands covered with the brown chili, was just standing there puzzled, and the thin woman on the couch didn't move. He looked at the doorway to the other room and saw the man from the loan company smiling, and he saw the smile change to a glassy look when their eyes met.

The large colored woman said, "Grandma takes funny things in her head once in a while." She peeked around the edge of the cushion, then put it back.

And the loan-man, with the yellow paper propped against the jamb of the far door and his pencil poised over it, kept staring. Charlie put up his hand to cover his mouth and nose, but the other man didn't shift his eyes. Well, he hadn't run far enough or long enough. People still read the newspapers, and his picture stuck in the backs of their minds, slotted in there with the brains and things. You could wiggle, jerk, fake the heebie-jeebies to keep your face changing, but their eyes moved so quick it didn't matter. He stepped to his right and got the bulk of Ada between him and the loan-man.

Ada said, "I hope that Kate's got a wash-machine. I can feel grease in this stuff." She rubbed her fingers together for a moment, then tried to wipe her hands clean on the bottom part of her dress, hiking it up till the lace edging of her slip showed.

Charlie said, "Let's go somewhere before it gets late."

After taking the cushion away from the window and speaking some low, tough words through it, the large colored woman walked over to Ada and stroked her arm. "I'm real sad about this. Wipe some on the clean side of the cushion. Grandma threw some more on it already." She held it up to show the streaks on the underside.

Ada mopped her hands and bent over to scrape the front of her dress on the rough material. "Much obliged, thank you. I've got kind of sweaty too." She blotted her forehead with the cushion.

By this time, the loan-man had come back into the living room a few steps. He said, "What was your name again, mister?" His narrow, pale face pointed at Charlie.

Hooking his fingers under the side of Ada's belt, Charlie moved toward the door to the restaurant, coaxing her with him. He knew all the symptoms: now was the time to go away if he was going to get a little head start.

Ada said, "You mean Mr. Rupp?"

The loan-man came toward them uncertainly, twiddling his pencil between his thumb and forefinger. "You sure about that?"

As she put the stained cushion on the floor, the large colored lady said, "You better get on about your business. You supposed to be listing household goods."

The loan-man came further and said in a louder voice, "Just wait a minute, Rupp, or whatever your name is. You ever had your picture—?"

The thin colored woman on the sofa said, "Pardon me."

Trying to haul her gently and evenly, Charlie got Ada to the door and felt for the knob. She was raising a little fuss about it, switching her head around to look at him, giggling a bit, asking what was the matter.

The loan-man said, "You stand still, mister, I'm telling you." He put his pencil behind his ear and walked over to reach around Ada. "Let's just make a phone call."

The large colored woman, taking him by the waist with both arms, tightened her squeeze so hard that the loan-man doubled over and started to holler. She twisted him to one side and marched him toward the other room, staggering when he lashed with his elbows.

Charlie got the door open and backed outside with Ada.

She said, "What's happening?"

Before he closed the door, he saw that the colored woman had made it to the other doorway, but couldn't get the loan-man through. He held onto the frame with both hands and kicked backward. All the children were gaping. Charlie said, "We're going to the party now. Has to be right away, or we won't get there."

Ada said, "All right." And she shouted good-by through the door as Charlie closed it.

He linked arms with her, pulled his baseball cap low, and limped from force of habit toward the front of the restaurant. There was lots of noise, and that was good: all the booths were filled with people, chewing, drinking, gesturing at each other, and in the slim lane between the counter and the booths, a dozen or more men laughed and joshed in clouds of cigarette smoke. But when he and Ada passed the beer-cooler at the rear end of the counter and came into general view, nearly all the talking shut off suddenly, and though Ada smiled and tried to be happy at everybody, Charlie felt like he was walking into a police line-up. He kept his head low and concentrated on the front door-knob, trembling at the touch of all the eyes as they swept him up and down, as they shaved the short bristles on his upper lip mentally and knew him, as they noticed the smeared chili on his jacket and made it hot again. Must've been crazy ever to come into a place that could get so busy.

Ada brushed several of the men with her skirt, but they slipped out of the way. A bent-over old man, wearing a clean apron, was standing on a stool behind the counter, his ear pressed against a table-model radio with no case, listening hard, and because he was near the door and separated from most of the others, he caught Charlie's eye as the last one who could get in the way.

Suddenly the old man stepped down from his stool and waved. "Hey, Mr. Bell. Listen here."

Laying the flat of his hand on Ada's back, Charlie propelled her out of the doorway and got himself around the swinging edge, feeling the latch hook at his sleeve. They knew his name, and from that it was only a step to catching hold of him. He hustled Ada to the car, got both of them inside, and waited while she hunted for the keys.

She said, "I had them right here. This is so exciting."

The old man had followed them out of the restaurant, and he came hobbling over the bare patches of dirt between the sidewalk and curb, waving one hand. Charlie locked the car door, stoving his thumb on the torn upholstery as he did so, and reached across to help Ada grope in her bag. The keys came jingling out, and before Ada could drop them or lose them again, he stuck them into the ignition, switched them, and told her to go.

With a rattling roar, the car yawed away from the curb, smacking the bumper of the car ahead of them, then swerved straight down the middle of the street, headed west.

Ada said, "I can't see very much."

He pulled out the light switch for her. "You don't have to go so fast. We don't want to hit anybody." The streets and sidewalks were flush with people, but poorly lighted; and the front tires of the car kept shimmying as though they were on crooked. "Turn left when you get a chance."

He couldn't figure it out. He was finally getting some of the sludge out of his brain, but it didn't help. The people in the restaurant must have known who he was all along, yet they hadn't done anything, hadn't shrieked or had fits, hadn't roped him up while he was asleep, hadn't hurt him. The large lady had grabbed the loan-man at just the right time, as if she'd known exactly what was happening. But the old man behind the counter had yelped out the name of a maybe-murderer where all the folks who read newspapers could hear it. Didn't make sense, after they'd gone along with him for so many hours.

He steered Ada past obstacles and around corners till they were driving east, then turned her onto South Parkway. It was the only street he knew that led far enough away. They zoomed by a large, bird-stained statue of somebody and angled left through a huge wooded park.

On a broad thoroughfare again, Ada relaxed and let the car go. "I can't imagine how you got this idea in your head, Mr.

Rupp." She chuckled and made her chin wag. "I don't even recollect your first name."

"What idea?" He hadn't been thinking. He wasn't aware of having any ideas, except of course the one that bit him in the throat and told him to run, when he couldn't run.

She came to a wide, easy fork in the road and nearly went down the middle into the shadowy bunches of late-evening picnickers, but he guided her to the right. She said, "It's real flattering-like, I'm sure. A widow woman ain't good at knowing how to act."

He said, "Yes." Where should he ask her to aim for now? He could probably risk a bus station somewhere, even a taxi out of the county, but he wanted to go as far as she would take him.

During the lull, she spun the wheel when he pointed and finally nosed the car out, rattling, onto the Midway past the University of Chicago. "There ain't no party, is there, Mr. Rupp?"

Startled, he looked at her. Her hair, from the recent dashing around, had become bushier, higher at the top, wider at the sides; and her small, thick glasses glittered halfway down her nose. He'd taken for granted, all along, that she would believe anything he told her. "No, there isn't." She'd find out soon enough anyway.

"Well, I knew it. You wouldn't ask me to no party on such short acquaintance." She nodded and smiled as they chugged through a stoplight at the last possible second. "That's why I feel so riled, Mr. Rupp." She added hastily, "In a good way."

He tried to think, but nothing came. Would she dump him along here? It wasn't likely that she could find a police station if she hunted all night.

She took her eyes off the road and leaned at him. "You've fell in love with me, now haven't you." She glanced at the windshield when they went through an underpass, but turned back again and ignored it. "I read all about you soldier boys."

Trying to slide further away from her, he only hurt his side with the arm-rest. The reek of chili filled the hot air in the car, and he lowered the window an inch, feeling a little nutty.

Ada turned right at the next stoplight when he pointed, and straddled the bumpy streetcar tracks on Stony Island down to 63rd Street where the tail-end of the Elevated stuck out over them. She said, "Well, to come right out with it, I ain't never eloped before, so you got to show me how to do it. Me and my husband was engaged for a real long time."

Though he was feeling feebler and feebler, Charlie tried to rally himself. You couldn't just let things like this happen for the hell of it. "Well, to tell you the truth—"

She let the car be nudged along by the traffic until they were on the southbound lane of the divided Stony Island. Sprinkled by the vari-colored neon lights of the used-car lots, she patted his knee. "I know. When you come flopping into our room at the hotel, I seen you'd caught me. It's all right. I accept. I'm only sixty-one, and we can have kids and all. Kids is nice to have."

His head simmered under his baseball cap, and he realized that some people could chase you without moving at all. You could sit still, refuse to play, go to sleep, and they'd scuttle after with their minds, grabbing. They crossed the IC tracks at 71st, but he didn't look left to try to see the record shop. "I never had any kids."

She said, "I had two, but they don't count."

Neither spoke for a long time, and the car wheeled and staggered at the messy intersection of Stony Island, 79th, and South Chicago Avenue, and when they finally wound up going southeast on South Chicago, Charlie didn't care. Any direction was the same. Maybe she'd get awfully huffy when he had to tell her they weren't eloping. Well, he'd just leave the car there and walk. She'd find something else to be screwy about. He couldn't work up enough of himself to feel sorry for her: she was too shifty at starting on new things. He watched a brilliantly lit gas station go floating by, all yellow and gabby with signs about oil, and he saw the safety islands, like long one-masted canoes, swish by the left fender and the people standing on them dance backward when Ada spun the wheel in time. He didn't feel afraid, just drained.

Ada said, "Do they have justice-of-the-peaces around here? I ain't got nothing against reverends, but my dress is kind of greasy." She took both hands off the wheel to pluck at the front of it. "How did that there chili happen?"

"I don't know." He didn't feel like explaining, and he especially didn't feel like getting married to anybody. Even *wanting* to get married was bad enough. That was how you learned to wake up in the morning with a bitter taste, like shaving lotion, in your mouth. You had to be an engineer, or almost, to get married, and he wasn't husky enough in the head to be an engineer, not even a diamond-burning fireman.

They passed a power plant with a fenced-in electrician's nightmare beside it, all wires and transformers, and as the street sloped and turned a little left, Charlie saw the railroad underpass like a dirty tunnel with concrete pillars in the middle. A long freight train was parked on it, engine chuffing steam out and down over the entrance, and Ada, catching the stoplight on green, let the car bump down the rough incline. When the car went into the steam, she took her hands off the wheel and laughed.

She said, "I'm just guessing now."

This was the closest he'd been to a train for what seemed like a long time, and he didn't like it, didn't like the enclosed rumble from overhead or the sense of being sat on. But instead of shutting his eyes to get rid of it, he grabbed the wheel and turned it in time to make the car miss the row of center supports that suddenly appeared in the dull glow of the headlights.

The car came out the other side slowly, rockily, and nearly stalled because Ada had taken her foot off the gas. She said, "Did we go through something?"

He couldn't find his voice. He merely pointed to the half-left turn leading to the bridge. Well, he'd find a bus station as soon as possible.

She shifted gears to go up the slope toward the bridge, and the car barged into the merging traffic when she trod on the gas and made the motor howl. "It's getting pretty hilly. Are we still in Chicago?"

"Yes." He watched the fire-working hulks of the big steel mills to his left near Lake Michigan and saw a block-long ore boat coming down the narrow, scummy lane of water toward the bridge. The red port light stared at him; the green starboard light winked into sight as they crossed the bridge; and then the red light disappeared as they went down the other side. Already the warning signals at the edge of the road had begun to clang and flash, and by the time they came to the pock-marked, half-brick, half-asphalt curve, Charlie saw, looking back through the dusty rear window of the car, that the gates were down and that the bridge was going up, breaking itself in the middle to let the ore boat through. How did the watchman there feel? He didn't like to think about it. At least, the ships and boats didn't make much noise.

Ada said, "You ain't talking hardly at all, Mr. Rupp. Are you scared?"

He said, "I don't think so."

"You still ain't told me your first name. No call to be 'shamed of it, whatever it is." She honked at a car that tried to pass her.

"It's—William."

She pumped the brake for a stoplight at a five-street intersection. "Well, isn't that a nice name. William." She pulled her dress down as far as it would go over her knees. "Ada Rupp. How does that sound?"

He lowered the side window another inch and unlocked the door.

She hummed to herself, squinting ahead at the many taillights. "It's kind of hard to tell which is the stop sign. I don't see no green anywhere." She hummed some more. "We just keep going straight?"

"Take the street a little to the right. Trucks don't go that way." He thought about it. The street would bring them to Indianapolis Boulevard, only a mile from the state line, and just a mile on the other side of that line was a big soap factory, a dozen or so sets of tracks, a watchman's shanty, and a small garage apartment that probably had blood on the floor somewhere. Well, they wouldn't cross the state line there. Maybe just head south on whatever miserable street he could find, get down through Calumet City and Lansing, then far away.

All the other cars started, and Ada crept along, hesitating, till he helped her pick out the quieter angle street that was straight and long. She got up a little speed and let the steering wheel jiggle negligently as they skimmed by the rows of parked cars and the blocks of frame houses. The night had seeped in more definitely here, had made the houses crouch, had taken over the mid-block sections and blurred them between the streetlights.

Ada said, "I don't like to bring this up so off-hand, but how long is your furlough, William, and have you got any money?"

He snapped nervously awake. "About twenty-five dollars." It was so hard to tell her what was really happening. He felt dirty and mean, and he began to phrase in his mind just the way to say it so she wouldn't cry or do anything like a woman.

She said, "Oh, that's plenty. Kate'll send me lots if I ask nice."

Hunching down and supporting his head by holding his finger under his nose, Charlie watched the pavement rush toward them and zig-zag into the front of the car. It would take some doing, but he could always walk away in the middle of a sentence and leave her hunting for him. Then maybe she'd make up a story in her head about his getting lost in the dark. She could call Kate and find out where Burnham or Lansing was.

Idly at first, then with more concern, he saw they were approaching another underpass, a short one, banked up on both sides to the high railroad tracks. Ada was letting the left tires of the car ride the center line of the street, and where the center line went through the underpass, another row of dull-gray concrete supports started. He said, "Get over to the right."

She took one hand off the wheel and slid six inches toward him on the seat. She laughed. "Okay, but remember we ain't married yet, Mr. Rupp."

The car was wiggling, still too close to the middle. "I mean on the road." He reached for the wheel.

She stuck her face close to the windshield as they came to the slim entrance. "Is they a stoplight? I can't see—"

He tugged at the wheel frantically, but the front of her was pressed against the spokes nearly hard enough to blow the horn, and he couldn't get it around soon enough. The fender on her side cracked against one of the support columns, the shock making him lose his grip, and then sideswiped another, still another, so fast that he couldn't count the noises, and Ada reared back away from the steering wheel. He covered his head with his arms and felt the car skidding and twisting, throwing out the sound of breaking glass, and he didn't open his eyes, because it was horrible enough to feel the lurch that rammed him over against the door and hurt his shoulder, and before he could think to cover up his legs too, he found himself tumbling sideways through the sprung-open door and rolling crazily in the street with his legs tangling together like strands of taffy.

He stopped when his hip bumped the curb, and he lay there, trying to remember something. There was something you weren't supposed to do, and he couldn't think of it. No more noise now, and as he took his arm away from his eyes and leaned on a sore elbow, he saw the car, still upright but turned perpendicular to the direction of the street, its nose against the support columns, front wheels sprawled flat, and one headlight on, bashed upward and aiming at the roof of the underpass. Light enough for seeing, but not enough for thinking.

He crawled up onto the moist sidewalk, trying not to use his unbelievably aching knees, and looked for Ada. She was getting out of the open door, rubbing her big chest, and when she stood on the pavement, he saw that one of her shoes was gone. She limped around in a small circle.

She said, "Mr. Rupp? You anywhere? I bust my glasses."

Another car had pulled up to the entrance of the underpass, and people were coming. He could hear them. He crawled over next to the wall on the shadowy sidewalk, using his hands and letting his legs drag. Everything had gone wrong with his legs, and soon there would be a million people nosing around, giving first-aid and things, and policemen with those notebooks. Flat on his stomach, he inched forward along the wall and away from Ada and the car. She'd be all right. Folks would take care of her, but he couldn't let himself be trapped in here, not when he didn't have a chance to run any more. It wasn't fair to be caught when you couldn't even walk away.

Somebody said, "What happened?"

Charlie, knowing his legs would be even worse after the first numbness wore off, forced his knees to help him crawl, and by the time somebody wearing a pink dress was standing beside Ada under the lopsided light, he had come to the end of the underpass. The sky was black, but the lights from cars coming toward him made things brighter than he wanted; so when the wall mooched down to the level of the sidewalk after six more yards, he reached over it, grabbed two handfuls of weeds, and gradually pulled himself in. He remembered swimming under water at Cedar Lake: how the tough green stems, rooted in mud, had raked at him when he tried to fight through; he'd had to use them hand over hand like a ladder to get anywhere.

He couldn't think straight, but he knew he was finished if he couldn't get out of here. More cars were stopping, lighting up the underpass like a carnival, and people from the stores at the next intersection were trotting along the sidewalk toward the wreck.

Soon they'd be hunting for him, because Ada would tell them all kinds of stories; and maybe she'd get her picture in the papers, looking big and happy, telling about Mr. Rupp who'd evaporated with the force of the crash.

There were strange messes in the weeds; he could smell them. Dogs had been there, and dead vegetables. He crawled up the slope toward the tracks because it was darker, and when the burrs and last year's nearly buried brambles scratched his face and caught in his hair, he realized that he'd lost his baseball cap somewhere. Using his elbows like crutches, he strained upward to the edge of the high roadbed where the cinders and fill-dirt started and the weeds ended, and he lay there wondering how many places his legs were broken in now. The pain was growing in them, and, remembering, he knew it could grow a long way yet. He didn't dare think of standing up to find out whether they'd bend in the middle.

Then long flickering minutes went by. The commotion down below got bigger, faded away, got bigger again. Once he lifted his head to the level of the weed tassels to see Ada's Plymouth being hauled away by a tow truck in the same direction they'd been going. He didn't see her. After that, most of the lights went somewhere else, and the irregular stream of cars dipped down and buzzed through the underpass as if nothing had happened.

But everything had happened. He didn't feel exactly sick or sleepy, yet he had a tendency to disappear in his mind, then suddenly pop back into being real. And his legs didn't hurt too much any more, really: he figured the nerves between them and his head must be pretty near shredded with all the messages they'd had to carry the last few days. What was most important was that he was stuck, rat-trapped with his face hanging out for anybody to see. To be able to trade faces in—that was it. Or better yet, to be able to cancel a couple days and hand them back for a refund.

He had cleared his throat, had propped himself up till he could see part of the sidewalk below in the alternately dim and brilliant light, and he had decided to shout at the next person who walked by there and take another useless chance; but a passenger train highballed from the east and rumbled past him on the further track only a dozen feet away. It didn't frighten him, not even the geyser of dead steam, trailing from the pistons, that dampened his face, or the hot soot that rained around, or all the noise, or the way the ground flapped, jarring his chest. He watched it go by and felt the trailer of wind curl over him as it followed the train toward South Chicago. Nobody got knocked out of the next-to-the-end door. No paper butterflies came out. Most trains weren't so bad after all, and nothing got hitched if they kept hurrying. Pausing or stopping was the trouble.

He forgot about calling to anybody on the sidewalk. Might be best to just lazy it until a lot later when only old guys walked the streets. You could halfway count on old guys. Somebody going to work who didn't have a chance to think very much, who used newspapers only for wrapping sandwiches to keep them from slopping around in the bucket. That kind of guy would know where to find crutches and an empty bedroom.

Twenty-five minutes of stirred-up pictures clacked through his mind and shifted. Lying in the wet weeds made him think of the farmland he'd thought of buying once below Crown Point. He'd liked the way the hills were wrinkled with green grass; not hills exactly, just dips and swells. But in his mind there were people all over it now, spoiling the smooth lines. Ada sprawled on her side, feeding a litter. The stocky man licking a salt-block. Lily laying an egg, sitting on it, squashing it. Old Mac ringing the bell around his neck. Clay climbing a tree. Dr. Chandler crying out loud. All of it had begun to be funny, after a while, and he kept his nose in the crook of his elbow to keep from being distracted; but when the ground started shaking again and he heard the ramming of steam, he sort of woke up and saw the eye of an engine growing in the west, and he remembered where it would be headed.

The chuff out of the stack was slow, even-spaced, and as the big drive-wheels ground by him, denting the rails, making the ties squeak, he kept his head pulled back into the weeds. This would take him a long way, past the soap factory and his shanty, past Gary, probably at least as far as Fort Wayne before a stop. If he could get on it, wedge himself in somehow, he wouldn't be taking any bigger risk than asking a stranger from the sidewalk below to help him. As soon as the coaler and the first five cars had gone slowly to the other side of the rail overpass, he crawled closer to the tracks, digging his fingers into the cindery embankment and lifting the toes of his shoes so they wouldn't drag too much.

He was scared now, but wouldn't think about it. The train was long and heavy, and when he pulled himself up close, using the tie-butts till his head was only a foot and a half from the drag bellies of the cars, he looked west and could barely see the crummy's lights. The raucous squeal of the wheels and springs set his nerves quivering, but he stayed there, bracing his arms straight under him, and tried to wait for a flatcar or an open freezer. He couldn't see very well—dust fanned him in the eyes—and when he felt his arms giving way, he knew he'd have to take the next one, whatever it was, or not make it at all. It was hard enough doing a flip in the best of times, but without legs, he'd have to be right the first try. As the car groaned past and he saw the grab-irons on the end of it coming, he rose to his knees, and using one hand for a fraction of a second, he pulled at his left leg till the sole of his shoe scraped up flat on the cinders; then in the only instant it could happen, he reached with both hands and thrust with his leg, and he hollered at the pain, choked at it, as his fingers caught the first iron above the stirrup. Momentarily he felt himself swept toward the rear of the train, and he tightened his hands till he couldn't feel them; then his feet began dragging along the tie-butts like sticks on a paling fence. Frenzied, he went up the ladder hand over hand to the third grab-iron, the fourth, his wrists clicking until he left the ground.

His legs swung forward again and hit the edge of the car. He looked down and wedged the toes of his safety shoes into the slot of the stirrup at the bottom, but he didn't dare put any weight on them, or the shock would make him lose his hold. He clung, as though trying to do an impossible chin-up, while the train rumbled over another street, cut into the darkness, and rolled onto the wide, wide maze of tracks that aimed southeast toward Indiana, less than a mile away.

He didn't belong on the outside of the car where the dirt could rush at him, where anybody who took the trouble to look could see him. He should be inside, or at least between, propped on the narrow death-woods above a coupling; but he couldn't move, and he knew it. He couldn't make it to Fort Wayne or Valparaiso, or even Gary or Whiting. He couldn't even make it to his own crossing, but he wanted to try. Maybe he could hole up in the shanty till morning, then figure something out. He tasted blood in his mouth, and he felt around with his tongue without finding a cut anywhere. Well, maybe he'd bitten himself.

Behind him and over the tops of short houses and buildings, he could see the garish bunches of light from the countless gas stations on Indianapolis Boulevard and could see the traffic whipping in both directions. Closer up, he couldn't see anything except an occasional gleam from another set of tracks or the humped groups of tumbleweed. He hissed through his teeth and made the bottom half of his body disappear. It wasn't any good anyway, gimping him, making him a flat wheel. But he couldn't make his nose fall off. It caught the rancid odor of cattle cars up ahead and made him dizzier, stuffed his head with dirty straw. And the only parts of his arms he could holler away were his fingers, stiff over the rung; his elbows grew knots on them. The train went a little faster, jerking itself from side to side, like a dream that wouldn't go the way you wanted it to.

He was almost sure he'd died awhile ago, and it was on a train, too, to fill in the circle for Lily and the rest of them. Nobody had been satisfied with him just working, not even himself, yet he'd never dreamed of the lousier things you could cram into your hours. But he wasn't dead, because he could still look with his eyes, stare through the streams of cattle-smell and see the soap factory poking up out of the dark like a yellow cloud. It came closer, but it didn't get any brighter; his eyes worked in loops and didn't let him get a straight crack at it. Well, he was going to get off here. When you couldn't run, walk, or stand, it was time to get tired and time to forget. He watched the weed jungle where he'd ducked the stocky man and the man who wasn't stocky, saw it rock past, and he saw his shanty four tracks over. Didn't have to worry about hurting his legs. Didn't have any legs. Good soft bank below to sleep in; and he shook his fingers loose and covered his head with his arms, waiting to fall and get killed again. When he started to swing backward, he didn't close his eyes. And he was looking, not quite horrified, at his scuffed safety shoes wedged into the stirrup, and as he pivoted on them in a crumpled somersault, watching between his arms, he saw his shanty spin up over the sky, then saw the dark fly up and turn into many, many circles.